Once Upon a Halloween Day
Short Stories

Tiffee Jasso

ISBN: 978-1-7350565-3-1

In memory of Gail Tiffee -Young. I would not have written these stories without your constant encouragement that I keep writing. When you passed this past year, I woke up the next morning, and realized that it was the first day of my life without you. After I shed a tear or three, a thought came to me, and I smiled. I have a library of memories of all the things we did, laughed at, and went to see in my mind. Also, my signed Animals Album by your friend Eric Burdon that you brought me. You always traveled the road and made loads of friends. Me, I traveled in my imagination and made friends of another kind. Between us both we shared a lifetime of tales and happiness. Until we meet again, dear sister, I will keep you in my mind and heart.

No Place to Hide

October 31, 1969, Bevinsville USA

The young man ran into each bar on the street, took a look around, and then ran back out. He was hunting for Joe Benson, the author of "No Place to Hide." He carried a ragged copy of the book in his hands as if it were a life ring in a raging ocean, and he was a drowning man.

As he neared the end of the street, he saw a red and blue neon sign advertising the Dead Pig Saloon. He bit his lip, and prayed the man would be inside. Time was running out. He had to find Benson, and soon. The monsters were killing people.

He entered the smoke filled room and spied a face that seemed familiar. He compared it with the face on the back of the book's cover. *Yes, that's him*, he told himself, and ran over to the table.

"Mr. Benson?"

"What's it to you, kid?"

"Did you write this book?" Claudius asked, holding the book up for the man to look at.

"So what? I don't give refunds."

Claudius shook his head. "No. I don't want my money back. I just need to know what you would do if the beasts in this book were real?"

Benson laughed uproariously at that question.

"That's the first time anyone has ever asked me that question. The book is fiction. You know, imagination.

Something from a nightmare. That is what I do as a writer."

"But what if they were real? What would you do?"

"What's your name, kid?"

"Claudius Stoneshell."

Benson paused to look at the young man. He had heard the name Stoneshell before but could not recall when or where. "Good solid name. I like it," he said, nodding at the young man.

"Mr. Benson. Time is running out. I need to know what you would do if the beasts you describe in this book were real?"

Benson sat back in his chair and looked at the kid. For the first time, he noticed how pale the kid's face was, and his eyes were filled with fear. "Okay, if you need to know. I will tell you but sit down first! My neck is beginning to pain me from staring up at you. How old are you? You seem pretty young to be in a bar."

"I'm older than I look," Claudius said as he sat down opposite the man he hoped was going to save the people of Bevinsville. "But I don't drink liquor. I don't like the taste of it."

"Well, good, because I don't think they would serve you in here anyway."

"Can you answer my question, Mr. Benson. I really need to know. Like, right now, *know*. Later, might be too late."

"Like I said, the creatures in that book are imaginary, but if they did exist, I would run to the nearest church, and get down on my knees before Jesus, and pray for God to help me because no one else could."

Claudius's face went white, and his eyes rolled slightly in his head.

Benson thought for a second, the young man was going to pass out. "Boy, when did you eat last?" he asked. "You look like you seen a ghost."

Claudius took a deep breath to clear his head. "Mr. Benson, we need to get to a church as fast as we can because earlier this evening, I seen a hole open up in the ground, and several beasts that look just like the ones you describe in this book, crawled out of it." Claudius held the book up for Benson to look at. "I imagine, they have killed quite a few people by now. Especially, the one that drinks blood by the gallon."

Benson blinked his eyes in surprise at the young man's claims. "You been smoking something?" he asked, looking to see if the kid's eyes were red.

"No, sir. I know what I saw."

Benson started to laugh, but stopped when a man ran in screaming that monsters had killed his brother.

Benson jumped up from his chair. Looked at the man, and then down at the kid. "You were telling the truth?"

Claudius nodded as he stood.

"Then follow me, boy! We got to run."

When Benson turned up the alley and started to run east, Claudius reminded him the direction to get to the church was the other way.

"Forget about the church, boy. That was hyperbole."

"Hyperbole?" Claudius asked, not familiar with the word.

"Yeah. You know? What a writer would do if they were writing a story. No church statue is going to stop beasts such as you describe."

"I didn't describe them. You did," Claudius said. "I have

3

never seen beasts like that in my dreams until I read your book."

"My beasts are fiction. Your beasts are alive," Benson shouted as he rounded a corner and then stopped abruptly, as he spied the three beasts coming up the street.

He put a hand over his open mouth as he gawked at the creatures. They sure did resemble the ones in his book, all right. Seven foot tall, ugly, huge furry chests, arms, and legs, all bulging with muscles, and black leather pants that were tore off at the knees. The largest one was green and had the same scar on its face as his character *Cryptsucker* did. The middle one, had a swollen looking club foot, covered in black fur just like his imaginary beast, *Boote*, did. The shortest one, he did not want to think about. If the beast was a real version of his character, *Damsol*, he was the worst of them all. His thirst for human blood was insatiable.

Claudius was not prepared for Benson's sudden halt, and he took evasive action to keep from slamming into him. "Sorry," he gasped as he bumped into the writer's arm. "I didn't expect you stop."

No Place to Hide
"Me neither, but as you can see, we need a new direction. Follow me, kid!" Benson hollered as he turned and sped off in the other direction.

When Benson spotted an alley, he turned down it, figuring he would put a block or two between them and the creatures. He was wrong, the alley was a dead end.

Benson panicked as he looked around. There were no doors to be found. He looked up and spotted a fire scape ladder. He ran toward it, jumped up to catch the bottom rung, then let his weight pull it down.

"You go first Claudius. There ought to be a roof door up

there somewhere. Find it and get it open because those creatures will be right behind us.

Benson had just pulled the ladder up behind him when the beasts turned into the alley. He forced himself to keep climbing, despite the fact his legs were shaking so hard he could barely get them to move. He almost fell as a scream ripped through the air. He looked up and saw a woman looking down at the creatures below, her mouth hanging open.

"Run, you fool!" Benson commanded as he pulled himself onto the roof and scrambled to his feet.

"Sorry," Claudius apologized as he opened the door to roof's stairwell, and held it open for Benson. "She was up here having a smoke. When I told her about the beasts, I thought she would run back inside, not go take a look."

"Never mind, just hold the damn door open!" Benson shouted as he pulled the fear-frozen woman along with him. As soon as he cleared the door, he shouted for Claudius to grab the woman, and get down to the next floor. He then shut the door and bolted it.

Benson hurried down the stairs to the next level. He bolted that door too. He knew the beasts would rip the doors open, easy enough, if they were the beasts from his book, but he hoped to slow them down long enough for him, the woman, and the boy to escape. When he spotted the elevator, he stopped.

"How fast does that elevator work?" He asked the woman, shaking her to get her attention.

"I don't know. It works like most elevators, I guess," she said as she jerked her arm away from him and began rubbing it.

"Well for your sake, I hope it does because we need to get out of here before those creatures decided to use us for appetizers."

Benson regretted his words as the woman's eyes rolled up, and she began to fall. He caught her and then, told Claudius to push the down button.

As he half carried and half dragged the woman into the elevator, he heard the pounding of feet, and the ugly noise of hinges giving away as they were ripped from wood.

Seconds dragged on while Benson waited for the elevator to close. He let out a breath of relief when he felt downward movement.

The woman moaned and opened her eyes. Once again, she pulled herself free of the man who held onto her and scowled at him.

"Do that again, and I swear I will leave you where you lay, lady. I don't have the time nor the energy to pack you around," Benson said gruffly, knowing it was an empty threat.

"My name is Betty Fisk. Who are you?"

"I'm Joe, and he is Claudius," Benson answered, figuring there was no need for last names as this was not the time or place for full introductions.

When the elevator's bell went off, and the door opened, Benson ran out into the hotel's lobby. A dozen or more people turned to look at them. Benson stopped.

"Look! I don't have time to explain it all, but there are several monsters on their way down the stairs. I suggest you all do what I am going to do—*run*! Maybe some of us will see the sun rise another day if we are fast enough."

When everyone just stared at him as if he had grown two heads, he added, "They eat people. Is that enough information for you?"

The author did not wait for an answer as he motioned for Claudius to follow him, grabbed up the woman's hand in his again, and dashed for the door.

The three of them ran a couple more blocks before Benson could go no further. He leaned against a block fence, grabbed his knees, and gasped for air.

Claudius stood there watching the man, concern on his face.

"Both of you go on," Benson said as he straightened up. For the first time, he felt the chill of the night air, and silently cursed his bad luck as he realized he had left his jacket on the chair in the bar. "I will catch up with you later."

Claudius shook his head.

"We cannot leave you here, Joe," the woman protested.

"Either you leave me here, or you die with me," Benson stated gruffly, not wanting to waste the few minutes of life he had left arguing with a woman.

As shots rang out, they all three turned to look behind them. The streetlights in front of the hotel gave them a clear view. What they saw terrified them all the more.

Betty cried out as she saw the monster snap the gunman's back over his knee, and then throw him down on the road.

Benson was surprised when none of the creatures paid any attention to the downed man. The Damsol in his book, would have immediately went for the man's throat. The three did pay attention to the two police cars with their sirens on that pulled up in front of them.

He watched with dread as the officers found their bullets had no effect, other than to make the beasts angry. When the beasts began moving toward the officers, both of them jumped into one of the police cars.

7

When the car began backing up, Cryptsucker and Boote, with the speed of the animals they were, picked up two nearby motorcycles and hurled them at the car. One motorcycle landed in patrol car's front window. The other motorcycle hit the roof, and then slid off to land behind the car where it jammed beneath the car as the wheels ran over it, stopping the vehicle's momentum.

"What are those things?" Betty asked, watching in horror as the patrol car ground to a halt.

"They are monsters from Mr. Benson's book," Claudius answered.

Betty's mouth dropped open as she looked at the young man. She shook her head. "Creatures from books don't come alive. If they did, we would all be dead."

"Damn straight, they don't!" Benson exclaimed righteously.

"Maybe so, but I saw them come from a hole in the ground at the cemetery, and they match the monsters in this book," Claudius argued as he held up the book.

"You never said they came from the cemetery," Benson said, giving the young man a scowl.

Claudius shrugged. "Does it matter?" he asked.

Benson scratched his head. "Hell if I know, but it probably has something to do with it. I think we better get to that cemetery and take a look at that hole."

"How did you get rid of them in the book?" Betty asked.

"A witch cast a spell that made them go back into the hole in the ground, they came out of," Claudius answered.

"Which does us no good as I am fresh out of witches," Benson snapped before he turned to look at the woman. "Betty you need to get out of here now!"

"My brother is at the National Guard building on B Street, and they have a couple of tanks there," Betty said.

"Good. Go tell him what has happened here, and make sure you get inside one of those tanks!" Benson ordered. "Flying motorcycles will bounce off those iron bohemoths."

Betty hesitated until she saw the monsters were again, headed toward them. "Take care!" she called out as she started to run in the direction of B Street.

"Follow her, Claudius!" Benson commanded when he too, saw the creatures coming their way.

"They might be your monsters, Mr. Benson, but they came from my dreams. I am sure you will think of something to save us. You always do in your books."

"Boy, where did you grow up? Characters in a book are words on a sheet of paper, not flesh and blood," Benson argued as he turned to look at the young man.

"I grew up in a cemetery," Claudius answered.

Benson spat out a curse as he eyed the young man. "No one grows up in a cemetery," he argued.

"Well, I did. My father was caretaker there until last year when he died. They buried *him* in the new cemetery. I am alone now."

"Sorry to hear that, Claudius."

"Yeah, me too," Claudius "It gets awful lonely."

Benson resisted the urge to pat the young man on the back to comfort him. Best to keep them as passing strangers, he told himself. He did not want the kid to mourn his loss too when his creations killed him. There was no doubt in his mind that was what they intended to do, and he had no way of stopping them.

The Cemetery

"Come on! Let's get to that cemetery and see if there is anything there to tell us what happened," he said. "If not, you have to go find Betty and her brother, and get yourself in one of those tanks."

"The cemetery is down that road," Claudius said, pointing at the next street.

"Yeah, I know where it is. I got family there too."

"I know—Joe and Martha Benson. I like the angel on Martha's headstone. That's where I found this book."

"I put that book there more than fifteen years ago. *No Place to Hide* is the first book I wrote."

"Oh, sorry. I thought someone lost it," Claudius apologized.

Benson shook his head. "It's okay, kid. When I put the book there, I was not much older than you are. At the time, it seemed important to let them know I had made it as a writer. I am past those days."

Benson saw the cemetery gates at the end of the street. He was too tired to run, and so hobbled along as best he could.

Claudius slowed down as well and stayed by his side.

"The hole is in the middle of the graveyard. There was an old oak tree growing there once, but it fell down last spring during a storm," Claudius said as he opened the gate, and then waited for Benson to enter before shutting it behind them.

Benson nodded. He recalled reading about the tree falling in the newspaper.

The old cemetery was beautiful in its own way, Benson thought. The elaborate marble and granite crypts and tombstones decorated with crosses, angels, flowers, hearts, scrollwork, and even a statue, here and there, were silent reminders of those who had come and gone.

He stopped before one of the elaborate graves with a rose bush arbor that still flourished. He saw the names Rose Marie Scranton, and baby Rose Marie, cut into the marble name plaque. Below that another name plaque had been added, some thirty years later, with the name Thomas Leroy Scranton, January 16, 1957.

Here lies the history of a family reunited in death. It is both a sad and a joyful tale, depending on one's perspective of death, he told himself. Then made a face as he found himself mentally storing that thought to use as the first line in his next story. Which was completely insane as there would be no next story. He would be dead within the hour.

He had never thought about where he would be buried, but now, he regretted that he would not be able to be buried near his parents. Instead, his body would be taken to the new cemetery with its one fountain, and hundreds of bronze and marble tombstones lying flat on the ground, like rectangles on a gameboard. No angels, stately statues, or urns. He would be just another blip on the ground. He shook his head at that thought. *That's the problem with being a writer, I am fluent in maudlin description*, he complained to himself.

"Mr. Benson, we need to hurry," Claudius called out when he realized the man was no longer following him. "The hole is this way."

Benson grateful for the interruption of his boggled mind, limped off in the direction the young man pointed.

When he came to the hole, he looked down into it, then stepped back and looked at Claudius. "I don't see anything down there that looks unearthly or evil. There's just dirt, and lots of tree roots."

11

"That's because that is not the hole they came from," Claudius said. "It is the one behind us. They came out of that crypt."

Benson turned and saw a marble crypt, it's stone door on the ground. His face lost its color, but it was not the pitch dark hole where the door had been that caused him to feel faint. No, it was the words on the granite name plaque on the left side of the door, *Claudius Roget Stoneshell, Born 1937-Murdered 1947.*

"That's your grave, isn't it, Claudius?" he asked.

"Yes, that is where I live. I told you I grew up in the cemetery."

"You did, but I thought you meant you lived with your father, not that you are a ghost."

"That's a *bad* word," Claudius said, glowering at Benson.

"Sorry, I did not mean to insult you, Claudius. I was just using the only word I know for someone like you."

"Do I look like any ghost you have ever seen?"

"Truth is, I have never seen one before."

"But your book has ghosts, witches, and monsters," Claudius accused.

"Yes, but they are not real, kid. They are only words on paper. You on the other hand, unless I am dreaming, are a real person despite the fact that you are dead."

Claudius's face broke into a smile at hearing he was a person. "I wish my father could hear you say that. He told me I had to hide or the man that killed me might come back and kill me again."

"Who killed you?" Benson asked, for the first time, considering the impact death would have on a ten-year old boy.

Claudius shrugged. "I don't know who he was, but I will know him if I see him again. He has a scar above his right eye, a black mustache, and a silver streak in his hair in his hair."

"Is the streak on the left side, about here?" Benson asked, as put a finger to his forehead.

"Yes, just like that. Do you know who he is?"

"Sounds like a man named Rom. He works at the Tit Tat, a bar on the other side of town. I go there sometimes. Why did he kill you?"

"It was late one night, and I heard strange noises coming from the graveyard. So I got up and came to take a look. He was breaking into a crypt of a woman who was buried earlier that day. Her grave is right over there in that big vault. The one with the angel on top of it." Claudius paused to point at a large crypt, a few rows up from his. "I saw him take the jewelry off her fingers, and a necklace off her neck. When I told him to put them back, he grabbed me. I started screaming, and he choked me so hard I could not breathe. I don't remember much of anything else, until I woke up one day. Father cried something terrible when he saw me come walking in. He said I had been asleep for ten years."

Benson felt his throat tighten with emotion as he listened to Claudius's account of his murder, and spiritual resurrection.

"If I live through this, Claudius. I will see if I can get the sheriff to press charges. I am not saying he will, as I dare not tell him the entire story, or he will think I'm crazy. You have to keep in mind there are very few people like you, walking around."

"I understand, Mr. Benson. Father said the same thing."

The hair on the back of Benson's neck rose of its own accord. He turned around and saw Boote, Cryptsucker, and Damsol—licking his lips—walking toward him.

Benson watched Claudius lay the book gently down on the flower pedestal that stood beneath his name plaque and turn toward the three creatures.

"Stop!" Claudius said as he raised a hand. "Mr. Benson is my friend. He knows who killed me, so the hunt is over," Claudius stated. "When I determine it is the right man, then as I promised, you three can take care of him."

Benson's felt his legs go weak from fear as Boote, Cryptsucker, and Damsol walked toward him.

Boote, being the leader of the pack, could not resist the urge to assert his authority, and so, without warning, put out a hand, and shoved Benson in the chest. The blow sent the author flying.

All three monsters went into the crypt howling with laughter.

"Are you, okay," Claudius asked as he knelt down beside the man.

"I'll live," Benson said as he struggled to sit up. "Why do they obey you?" he asked.

"They are my pets," Claudius answered. "I created them with my mind from the characters in your book. I just wanted to meet you and show them to you. I did not realize they would kill people."

"They are killers, *Claudius*. That is what they do. Did you not understand that part of the book?"

Claudius lower lip curled up. "They are my friends. They did not kill anyone, until they were attacked," he said stubbornly.

"That may be, but killing people is never right. "Look at what it did to you. You have to get rid of them!"

Claudius cast the author an angry look. "No!" he shouted before he ran toward the black hole in his crypt.

Benson watched the kid's figure enter the inky darkness and disappear.

As he stood there wondering what he should do next, he heard sirens in the distance. The sheriff and others would be here soon. He knew that no matter how he rehearsed it, no one was going to believe his story. The truth would get him ridiculed before it got him arrested or sent to an institution for being insane.

"Don't come out of there, Claudius, until everyone is gone! And if you want to keep your pets, make them smaller," he shouted. "Oh, one other thing. Have them put that door back, so no one will try and get inside."

"There was no answer, but then, he had not expected one. He could only hope the kid heard him, and stayed where he was.

The writer recalled he had passed a bench a few rows back and went to find it. His ribs and feet hurt.

As he sat there, his story came to him. He had followed the kid into the cemetery to look at the hole the monsters came out of. While he was standing there looking at tree roots, the young man ran off toward the river. The monsters ran after him. His story would ring true, as it was the truth for the most part. All he had to do was leave out the ghost part, and it would match Betty's statement. When they did not find the boy or his monsters, they would assume he had either been killed or drowned, and so had the creatures.

Benson heard stone being moved and snuck a peek. The stone on Claudius's crypt was back in place.

Just in time, he thought as he saw Sheriff Tucker, and several of his deputies running towards him.

The End

The Birth of Jazz

New Orleans, October 31, 1907
Beauregarde Cemetery

The icy mist caressed her face as if she were one of its own children. The early morning breeze moved the dead leaves restlessly around her bare feet while the chain around her waist, being an inanimate object, held her unconscious body up against the ancient gravestone. Maple Lee—for that was the young girl's name—shivered in her blue-flowered flannel nightgown but did not wake.

A grating noise echoed as a stone slab in the base of one of the cemetery's marble tombs was pushed open on its invisible hinges. A furry scarred face appeared as the cave demon Buchwald stuck his head out and looked around. His violet flame-colored eyes pierced the mist as if it were not there. He jerked his head to the left when a rat scampered from one tombstone to another. Buch licked his lips, disappointed that he had no time to hunt for a snack. Not if he wanted to live, and he did. The witch queen Reggara, expected them back with the girl within the hour.

"What do you see, Buch?" Beastymoin asked, pushing impatiently on his brother's back.

"It's dark, what do you want me to see?" Buch replied with a chuckle as he crawled out of the hole before Beasty thumped him on the head.

"Where do you think he put her?" Beasty questioned as he followed Buch down one of the rows between headstones.

"Probably off by one of the fences. He's not keen on graveyards. You know? Afraid of ghosts he is," Buch said.

"Ghosts?" scoffed Beasty. "Why would anyone be scared of them? They are nothing but cold air when it comes down to it."

"He's scared of us too," Buch added with a grin.

"Ah. Well, he should be," Beasty said complacently. "We are much more dangerous than any ghost."

"Yeah, we may be full of air too, but it packs a lot more oomph!" Buch broke wind with an odorous rumble to make his point.

Beasty roared with laughter.

"Quiet fool! Someone might hear you," Buch said as he shoved one of his foul green hands over Beastymoin's face.

"Who would be out here in the middle of the night?" Beasty asked once he had removed Buch's hand from over his mouth.

"The Collector," Buch whispered.

That shut Beasty up. He had only seen the Grim Reaper one time, but it still gave him nightmares. Those horrible burning eyes had pinned him to the ground as he felt his breath leaving his body. He figured he would have died right then and there, but Buch had grabbed him by the arm and pulled him back in the tunnel beneath the tomb, breaking the death spell.

The Young Saxophone Player

Domino Beaker, a young man who could not pay his gambling debts, had been snoozing against a different tomb, one closer to the front gate, when Beastymoin's eerie laughter woke him. He opened his eyes and looked around worriedly. The mist limited his vision, and he could not see the two cave demons pass nearby, but he heard their footsteps and voices.

Who-Who but me would be in the cemetery at this hour? He asked himself as he tried to calm his racing heart.

He reached for his father's pocket watch, but his hand was shaking so bad he could hardly read the dial. He took hold of the watch with both hands and caught a beam of moonlight as it broke through the ancient oak tree above his head. He saw it was two thirty-two in the morning. Three hours to go before Earl returned, and unlocked the iron shackle from around his ankle, so he could go home. He stifled the urge to moan his misery as he put his watch away. He did not want whoever or whatever, was walking around out there to hear him, and come take a look. They might not be friendly. Especially when they saw he was a black man chained to a tomb in a white-folks cemetery.

Domino shivered, drew up his legs, and wrapped his arms around himself. It was damp and cold. He was glad he had borrowed his father's old dark navy blue wool pea coat to wear to work, nights were getting cold. Of course he never expected to be using it for a blanket in a graveyard.

I told you to go straight home, his mind scolded. *You'd be in your own bed right now if you had listened. But you decided to play with the dice and lost."*

As the voices went off in another direction, Domino slumped with relief against the tomb's marble base, but all thoughts of trying to catch a nap was gone. He was wide awake, scared to the bone, and beating himself up for gambling with real gamblers. By the time he had found the markers were dollar ones, and not penny ones, it was too late. He only had twenty-five cents in his pocket, and he owed Big Nate two dollars.

When Big Nate saw he could not pay, he had grabbed him up by the collar, slapped his face hard, and then asked those standing around watching, "What should we do to this horn playing rat who cain't pay his gambling debts?"

Domino swallowed back the tears as he recalled how one of Nate's men had taken his knife out of his pocket, and suggested they make a few cuts here and there. "Mo' there... than elsewhere," the man had drawled, leering as he pointed the knife at the section of his body just below his belt.

Everyone had thought that was funny and laughed.

"Nah, he's old man Jake's boy, I don't want to cripple him, just teach him a lesson," Nate said before he slapped the other side of Domino's face just as hard as he had the other side.

Then put him in the graveyard for the night," someone shouted. "Maybe, he will meet up with some spooks. That'll teach him."

"If he lives through the night," Earl the bouncer sniggered. "They been some spooky things going on in that graveyard. Ah've heard the screams."

"That's a good idea," Nate said, "considering its past midnight, and today is Halloween. They say ghosts come out and dance on Halloween."

Domino felt lightheaded as Nate shook him like a rag doll, and asked, "Ya'll feel like dancing, Domino?"

Everyone belly-laughed again.

Someone had tried to take his saxophone away from him, but Nate shook his head, and held onto the horn until the man let go. "That horn is his saving grace. The boy can play it like Gabriel, himself. Earl, you take him over to the graveyard, and see that he stays there! And don't you be hitting him on the mouth! The boy has to be able to blow his horn tonight. The customers like his music."

Domino moved to stretch his shackled leg out, but the chain stopped him as it wasn't long enough. Tears came to his eyes as he shivered, more from fear than weather. He wiped them away using a coat sleeve. He felt the clammy dampness of the mist on the wool and felt colder for it.

The Young Girl

The two demons found the girl by the southeast corner of the cemetery and used the iron key the witch queen had given them to open the lock. They quickly freed the girl from the stone and carried her limp body toward the entrance to their underground realm.

Domino heard voices again. This time they were arguing softly and moving his way. *Lawd stay with me, and I promise not to gamble with the dice, no more,*" he silently prayed.

The seventeen-year-old musician reached over, and picked up his saxophone, intending to use it as a weapon to protect himself, if needed.

"Let's put her down for a minute, I need to rest," Buch said as he lowered the girl to the ground.

"Whew! About time. My arms hurting," Beasty complained, letting the girl's feet fall toward the ground.

The cave demon did not worry about her waking up, she had been given a potion that would keep her asleep.

Domino risked a peek and saw two short ugly looking furry creatures with horns on their head standing over a white girl-child that couldn't have been more than ten years old. At first, he thought the girl was dead, and the beasts had stolen her from one of the graves, but then he saw her chest heave, and she moaned softly. He knew she was still alive. He ducked back behind the tomb and prayed the two beasts had not seen him.

"Which parts do you think she will give us to eat, Buch?" Beasty asked.

Buch glowered at his brother. "Probably not more than a couple of toes or some fingers," he answered as he looked at the sleeping figure.

Domino almost swooned at those words. His body shook so hard the chain around his ankle clinked. Domino grabbed his leg and held it down to the ground. Fortunately, an owl hooted about that same time, and so, neither cave demon paid the noise any attention.

"But we do all the work," Beasty protested.

"Won't matter. This one is a bit smaller than the one last year, and she only gave us a foot to gnaw on from that one."

Stand Up!

Domino's heart thudded in his chest as he listened to the pair discuss the girl's fate. The hand that held his saxophone was clenched, so tightly against it, he felt his muscles protest. He looked at the instrument, and then toward the front gates. If he blew his horn, maybe someone would hear him, and come running, he told himself.

That might happen. Then again, maybe no one will come, and they'll eat you too," the part of his brain that was scared said.

Don't matter, we cain't allow them to eat that girl, he told his cowardly side. He put the horn to his lips, but his mouth and throat muscles were so paralyzed with fear he could not get his lips to make a circle so he could blow.

"Lawd, help me!" He silently cried out, panic, setting in.

"STAND UP!" a voice in his mind shouted. *"You cannot fight them sitting on your backside. Nor can you blow your horn loud enough to be heard."*

Domino jumped to his feet and frantically tried to think what song he should play.

"SONG?" The same strong voice shouted at him again. *"Forget that! Make that horn screech like you never have before, boy! Wake up the dogs, and you will wake up the people."*

Domino put the most effort he had ever put into blowing his horn. He hit notes he did not know he had. His horn bleated out C, D, B-flat, and kept on going up until it shrieked like a chalkboard being scraped by a split-cane rake. Dogs barked, and cats ran as the harsh sounds bombarded their ears. Chickens on their roosts squawked, and backyard pigs squealed. Folks up and down the street woke up and ran to take a look out their windows.

To the Rescue

"Well, I guess we had better go see what trouble Domino's gotten himself into this time. We don't want anyone finding him chained to that tombstone. They might hang him for trespassing, and that would upset Nate," Earl said when he heard the horn blowing. He threw his losing poker hand down on the card table.

With a few impolite remarks, the other two men who worked for Big Nate—Blinky, and James—threw their hands in as well, and went to put on their coats.

* * *

Beastymoin jumped a foot or more in the air as the horn sounded, and turned to run, but Buchwald reached out, and grabbed his arm before he could move, and stopped him. "Grab the girl, Beasty! We need to get out of here," he said as let go of his brother, and lifted the girl up by her arms.

"Leave her, Buch! It's the Collector," Beasty cried as started to run.

Buch dropped the girl and grabbed his brother.

"No, it's just the caretaker," Buch told him disgustedly. "Help me shut him up!"

Beasty reluctantly followed Buch around to the other side of the tomb. He took a good look at the tall, black man with a brass horn sticking out of his mouth standing in the mist, and decided Buch was right, it was not the Collector.

Domino's eyes were frozen on the two creatures, but his lips and breath never stopped. His horn screeched up and down the scale as fast as he could go.

* * *

Earl picked up his feet as the horn got more raucous. Something had Domino worked up and it did not sound good. He began to run. The others followed.

"I told ya'll he'd not sit the night through," James complained. "But I sure hope he ain't seen a real ghost. Cause if he has, ah'm not going in there."

All three men stopped mid-stride as the horn stopped abruptly. Then they heard Domino's high pitched screams. Earl picked up his feet and began to run toward the cemetery. Blinky and James reluctantly followed him, knowing Nate would fire them if Earl got hurt.

Change of Plans
Buch and Beasty had Domino on the ground trying to get around the horn the man was using to defend himself, out of the way, so they could take a bite out his neck.

Buchwald's ears rang as the man let out another high-pitched screech. He bit down on the man's arm, but instead of causing any real injury, he got a mouth full of damp wool which he nearly choked on.

Beastymoin went flying in the air as Domino's leg, the one without the chain, connected with his belly. When he got himself up off the ground, he saw a group of men running towards them. He hurried over and grabbed Buch off the man, pointing toward the men.

Both cave demons fled back to the base of the tomb, and quickly dove into the tunnel.

Buchwald grabbed the door and pulled it shut, making sure to lock the magic latch. It would seal the door cracks, making the stone seamless. He stood there breathing loudly as he looked at his brother, panic on his face. Without the girl they were dead beasts.

"I think it's time we went and visited Uncle Dobswort, in Charleston," he told Beasty. "If we go back without the girl, it will be us that Reggara will put in the pot."

Beasty nodded. He knew Buch was right. They would have to find a new home, and a faraway one at that. The witch queen's magic was only good in her realm. As soon as they crossed the line into the next realm, they would be safe. Good thing Buch always carried a tunnel map with him, he told himself. His empty stomach growled in hunger, but he told it to shut up as he followed Buch down into the underground maze below the graveyard.

Saved

Domino broke down and cried when he saw Earl had come to save him. "I thought they had me for shore," he said between sobs. "They were some kind of devil creatures with horns, and eyes that lit up like fire. They tried to *eat me*."

Earl and the rest of the poker group had been too busy running to find out what was wrong with Domino that they did not realize the sheriff, and his deputy, were right behind them.

"What's going on here?" Sheriff Cotton asked gruffly, pointing his gun straight at Domino.

"Don't shoot me, Sheriff Cotton! I ain't done nothing wrong. I was just trying to save the girl," Domino pleaded, feeling lightheaded as he saw the barrel of the gun, and the sheriff's finger on the trigger.

"What girl?" Earl, and the others questioned.

"The one behind this here tomb," Domino said, sitting up, and peeking around the corner. He began to cry when he saw her laying there.

"What's that?" James asked as he spotted the small night gowned figure lying on the ground.

"A white girl!" Blinky exclaimed as he stared down at the child.

"Is she still alive?" Domino asked. "The creatures they had a hold of her."

Sheriff Cotton bent down and felt the side of the girl's neck. "She's alive, but she's colder than my pistol," he said, putting his gun away as he rose. "You, Earl, carry her seeing how you're the biggest one here! We'll take her up the street to Doc Farland's house."

"I'd like to carry her. Sheriff, if ya'll let me. I can wrap my coat around her," Domino said as he pushed himself to his feet. "That ought to help warm her a bit while I carry her to the doc's house. They were going to eat her, Sheriff," Domino added, tears leaking down his face.

Tobias, the graveyard's caretaker, came up with his lamp and held it out towards Domino. That was when all of them saw the condition of Domino's face and coat.

"Give the girl to him, Earl!" Sheriff Cotton ordered. "Looks like he's earned the honor of saving her, the hard way."

Earl traded the girl for Domino's horn, handing the instrument over to Blinky. He then scratched his head as he tried to figure out what to do next. It was going to be hard to explain why the boy was shackled to the iron work.

"What ya'll waiting for?" Sheriff Cotton asked when no one moved to follow him.

Earl took a big iron key out of his pants pocket. "Now don't take this the wrong way, Sheriff Cotton, suh. We were just having a bit of fun with the boy," he said as he bent down, and unlocked the shackle.

Sheriff Cotton's brow raised as he looked around at the men standing there. His gray mustache twitched a time or two to show his irritation. "Once we get the girl settled with Doc, ya'll can tell me what Domino's doing here chained to this here grave?"

"I lost a bet, Sheriff Cotton," Domino quickly put in, not wanting anyone to get into trouble.

"Don't want to hear a word about it, boy! Not until I get out of this fog, and back to my office where it's warm," Cotton said, holding up a hand to stop Domino. "I will then decide whether to arrest the lot of you. Henry you walk behind us and shoot anyone that tries to run! Got that?"

"Yes, suh," Deputy Henry Lester answered.

Earl, Blinky and James hung their heads, and silently followed behind Domino.

Rewarded

Domino sat on the front porch steps of his parent's one room cabin, looking at the dents in his horn. He blew a C note. When it sounded as clear as it always did, he blew a sigh of relief. If he had no horn, he had no job.

He took a piece of soft rag from his pocket and tried to polish out the scratches the creature's claws had made in the metal. The brass did shine, but the scratches stayed where they were.

He looked up as a fancy carriage stopped in front of the yard. His eyes rounded with surprise when he saw a white man in a fancy suit, step out of the carriage, and start up the walk toward him.

"Are ya'll, Domino?" the man asked.

"Yes, suh," Domino answered, jumping up, and giving the man a slight bow of his head.

"Sit, boy! You look like you done tangled with a bear."

Tears came to Domino's eyes as he thought of the two creatures that had attacked him. "Weren't no bear, suh. It was graveyard demons."

"So I heard. I'm Cyrus Townhouse," the man introduced himself, noting the look of terror on the young man's face as he spoke of the beasts he had encountered. "The Sheriff told me it was you who saved my little girl from those beasts. I cannot thank you enough for that.

Domino looked at the man with surprise, and then nodded, too shy to brag on what he had done.

Cyrus pulled an envelope out of his pocket and handed it to Domino. "Here's a small reward for your bravery. From the look of your face, I'd say you earned it, and more," he said, putting the envelope in Domino's hand.

Domino put his horn down and opened up the letter. He started to pull the card out but spotted what looked like a gold piece. His eyes went wide, and he looked up at the man. He started shaking his head. "I cain't take money for saving that po' girl, suh. The Lawd was the one that helped me do it."

Cyrus laughed at the young man's refreshing honesty. "Yes, I imagine he did, but my Grandfather said to give you that twenty-dollar gold piece," he fibbed, knowing the boy would not go against an elder's wishes. "I don't think either of us wants to tangle with that old man. Do we?"

Domino shook his head. "No, suh," he agreed, thinking of his own grandfather.

"Good. Cause I would like to get on home."

"What's her name?" Domino asked shyly. "She never did wake up and tell me."

"Maple Lee," Cyrus answered. "Named after her great grandmother, Maple Lee Beauregarde," he added before he turned to leave.

Domino's mouth dropped open as the man walked away. The Beauregarde's were the richest folk in town. He looked down at the coin in his hand, his eyes tearing up as he gave silent thanks to God for being alive, and for the gold coin.

He got up and went into the house to give the money to his mother. Times had been hard for them this past year, since his father's legs had been crushed by a crate that fell from one of the dock cranes, and he could no longer work. Twenty dollars, added to what money he could make with his horn, would help get them through the worst part of winter.

New Sound

Despite his injuries, Domino made it to the club a few minutes early. He put his coat on the door peg, and then stepped back to look at the patches of light blue cotton sacking his mother had used to repair the damage made by the demons. "They's victory patches, son," his father had said when he caught his son staring at his mother's repair work. "Not many can say they grappled with the devil and won."

Once everyone in the band heard the story, and looked his cuts and bruises over, they marched out on the stage. Domino followed them, and saw the club was overflowing with folk.

Big Nate rushed up to the stage and motioned for Domino to come forward. "These folks have come to see you play. They heard about you saving that little girl. How's your horn? Without waiting for an answer the big man continued, "I want you to play, 'When the Saints go Marching In,' like you never played it before. Can you do that? Your face looks pretty raw."

Domino swallowed nervously. He could play the song all right, but he had never had so many people staring at him. His mind told him not to worry, he would do just fine. "Mama put some gator grease on it. Don't hurt that much now," he answered.

"Good. Then ya'll can start playing as soon as ya'll ready," Big Nate said as he turned to look at the other members of the band.

Domino waited for his boss to get back to his table before he turned and looked at the man sitting at the piano. He moved closer to the other musicians. "You heard?" He asked and waited for the others to nod that they had. "Then how about we pick up the beat a bit and do a repeat of the chorus like we did last week when we practiced in the barn."

"You play, we'll follow," Rolly told him, striking a few keys on the piano to show he was ready.

The other band members looked at Domino with grins on their faces. That session of free play had surprised them all.

And so that night, Big Nate's Club, located in the French Quarter on Bourbon Street, became one of New

Orleans first night spots to bring a new sound to the city. One that would eventually become known as Jazz.

Domino went on to play at the club a night or two a week for years, but he took the job of groundskeeper Mr. Townsend offered him. The job came with a four room house and a garden plot.

Sheriff Cotton's Report

Sheriff Cotton read the note that came by Special Delivery. It was from the Governor's Office. He then had Henry Lester set down with pencil and paper to write a new report on the kidnapping of the Townsend girl.

"Make sure you get this down just like I tell you, Henry! This report is going straight to the Governor."

"Yes, sir," Henry said as he touched the paper in front of him with the pencil's tip.

"At about 3:00 AM, on October 31, 1907, myself, and my deputy Henry Lester responded to a horn being blown nosily at the local cemetery," Cotton began.

He went on to describe the beasts as best he could recall about finding the unconscious girl lying on the ground. He added that the prank being played on Domino Beaker, had saved the girl.

"Had the boy not been where he was, the girl would have disappeared, and no one would have known what had happened to her," he explained. "For that reason, I'm not pressing any charges against those who put him there as a prank. What has me worried, is we might have another Voodoo woman in town. I am sure you recall the problem we had with River Mary, and those walking dead men she created, a few years back," he said, reminding the governor of another incident involving witchcraft.

Henry Lester's face paled noticeably, and the pencil in his hand slipped a bit on the words, *dead men*, but he finished the report. He also made sure not to ask any questions about the River woman. He would have a hard time sleeping as it was. He had seen the fire in those creatures' eyes, and the horns on their heads with his own eyes.

"It is my opinion, it was the Townsend's groundskeeper that kidnapped the girl, drugged her, and put her in the cemetery, as he left town right after she was rescued. I have had Wanted posters made and sent out to nearby Parishes, warning others to look for the man, and will include a copy of the poster with this report for your record department," Cotton finished.

"I will make a copy, and get this out in the evening mail," Henry stated.

"Good. Because I would shore like to put this one behind us. Makes me nervous every time, I think about it," Cotton said.

"Me too," Henry agreed as handed the paper over for the Sheriff to sign.

The End

Halloween Skull Flash Story

October 31, 2004
Small Town in Arizona

Emily, I found a carved rock skull in a cave today. I wish you could see it in person, and not just the photo in this email. It radiates every color in the rainbow. It practically glows as if there is an inner energy inside it. The stone appears to agate with opalescent striations. I believe that is what makes it glow in the light. I am going to take it over to Doctor Ralph at the University. He may be able to tell me the age, and something about the people who carved it, Dan wrote.

I never expected to find something like this at my dig site, Emily. Pottery shards, broken tools, arrowheads, and maybe, a turquoise or bone fetish, but not a crystal skull. Maybe if I was in Mexico or Peru, but not here in Arizona. I was digging into a small cave I found just north of my dig site. I was about to quit for the day when I saw something sparkle. Needless to say, my heart rate went up as I carefully uncovered the face and saw this glowing macabre mask staring up at me. It took several hours to get it free of the dirt that surrounded it. Oddly enough, there was no dirt inside the skull, despite the open eye sockets and nose hole.

Whoa! the eyes just lit up. Or at least I think they did. There was a flash of light in the room, but I don't see it right now. It must have been a reflection, bouncing off the mirror behind me as a car passed by outside.

Finding a crystal skull is every archaeologist's dream. Finding a three foot hairy-spider that my roommate Chuck, hung over my computer for Halloween, not so much. Every time, I lean forward, its tangles up in my hair. It is an ugly thing with eight glassy eyes, and long wiry legs. If I did not know better, I would say it has grown several inches since I sat down here, but of course that is just my imagination working overtime.

I will tell you everything I learn when I get back from the University. Love you, Dan.

* * *

Twelve years later, Emily was going through some old papers when she found a copy of the email, and the photo of the skull Dan had found just before he, the skull, and half the people in the apartment complex he lived at, disappeared.

Tears filled her eyes as she looked over and saw the picture of her brother on her dressing table. The News people called it another Arizona mystery that no one seems to be able to solve.

Emily sighed, and started to put the copy of the email and photo of the crystal skull back in the box, but then stopped as she asked herself, why she kept them? When she could come up with no plausible reason, she tossed them both in the trash pile. Dan was never coming back.

The End

Purple Magic

Part 1

The Pumpkin Patch

It was two hours before daylight, and a damp mist covered the ground. The moon had long been swallowed up by storm clouds. A harsh cry broke the silence of the darkness.

"Hush, girl!" the old woman hissed. "Ghosts and demons roam freely tonight. It is All Hallows' Eve. If they find you giving birth in this pumpkin patch, they will attack. If the farmer comes, he will call for the Queen. Either way, we could lose the child and possibly our own lives."

Mary clamped her jaws shut, but still, a deep moan of pain rumbled out of her as her baby was finally born.

"It's a man-child, granddaughter, with a crown of dark hair," Granny announced in a whisper as she cut the cord. "Should he be blessed with magic, the Queen will take an interest in him. No doubt about that."

"I'll not be giving my child away!" Mary protested as she sat up and made a grab for her son.

"That is not how it works," Granny said, relinquishing the child. "The Queen has no interest in raising a babe. No, she will wait until he becomes of age before making him a Palace Mage, and then only if he has exceptional magic. It is our job to raise him properly."

"Oh, you can be sure of that. I will teach him to hate magic and mages."

Granny Hobb's blue eyes flashed with anger. "Then you might as well strangle him right now. It would be better for us all."

Mary began to wail.

"Quiet, girl! You will wake the dead, and then I will have to deal with them," Granny admonished.

Mary's cries stopped abruptly. She was terrified by the thought of the dead rising from their graves. Her parents had been killed by such creatures the night she was born.

"Pick a name for the child, Mary! I need to announce his birth to the stars," Granny commanded before she took the infant and wrapped him in a wool blanket. It was cold enough that she could see her breath.

Mary closed her eyes as she searched for a name. Then it occurred to her. She would name the boy for where he was born. Somehow, she knew it would make him stronger. "Pumpkin," she declared. "Just Pumpkin, nothing more. He has no father."

Granny shook her head. "You are both a blessing and a curse, granddaughter, but your choice it is. If he survives that name while growing up, he will be all the stronger for it."

Granny Hobbs got to her feet. She then took the babe from her granddaughter and held him up in the air. "To those who watch over us, on this All Hallows' Eve morning, I present to you this fine lad, Pumpkin."

Granny's deep blue eyes rounded as a purple light stirred the mist, then surrounded the babe. Purple was for the highest order of magic. Not for the first time, she wondered who the father was. Mary claimed to have no memory of the man.

She cradled the boy in her arms and looked down into his dark eyes. "Pumpkin, I have no doubt you will turn our world upside down."

Granny had no idea of how prophetic her words would be. Pumpkin would change their world in ways that his great-grandmother could not begin to understand.

Mary sat up as a large white owl with a black face and leg feathers circled them before landing on one of the larger pumpkins.

"Rise, girl, and bow before the Watcher of the Woods, Lord Otar," Granny commanded, waiting for Mary to stand before she handed the babe to her granddaughter.

Mary took her son and held him close to her breast as she bowed before the owl.

"*You must flee with your child,*" Otar said, speaking to both women with his mind.

"Why?" Mary asked.

"*There are those who will hunt you down once they learn a newborn mage with purple magic has been born.*"

"Why?" Mary repeated.

"*You would try my patience with your ignorance, woman, if I did not know that you are innocent. I say that because I know you have no memory of him that fathered the child. But know that this baby has been born with magic of the highest order. Some will consider him a threat and will not hesitate to have him killed.*"

At the owl's words, Mary's face lost color. "Where would I go? I have no skills other than spinning wool which pays only enough to help feed us. The only home I have is my grandmother's farm. I have no magic to protect us."

The owl blinked his large gold-colored eyes as he thought that over. "*I will cast a spell of invisibility upon the child for the first dozen years of his life. No one but you,* your grandmother, *myself, and my mate Tifa will be able to see, hear,* or sense him. *If someone asks you about the babe you carried, tell them he disappeared right after he was born. Since that is the truth, no deception in what you say will be found.*"

Otar did not add that he would make sure rumors of the babe's abduction were spread widely about the land.

"Thank you," Mary said, tears springing to her eyes.

"*Do not thank me, Mary. The child will still be a fledgling in human time when the spell expires. On that day, his magic will be felt by many throughout the realm, and he will need to be ready to use that magic to battle those who would want him removed from this world.*"

Otar turned to look at the grandmother as he unfolded his wings in preparation to take flight. "*Teach him well, Granny, if you would see him live to become a full-grown man.*"

Granny Hobbs had just enough time to nod and make a quick bow before the owl lord disappeared into the darkness of the forest behind them.

She waited a few seconds to see if he would return. When he did not, she motioned for Mary to move off the ground cloth she stood on.

"Best you go get seated on the cart, Mary. We need to get home before the midnight hour," Granny said as she picked up the birthing cloth. She would burn it in the laundry stove as soon as she got home. No one could know a child had been born in the pumpkin patch this day.

Characters

Granny (Irene) Hobbs: Grandmother to Mary Hobbs. Eighty-four years of age. Blue eyes. long silver-gray hair braided and tied with blue or red fabric. Small boned and thin despite her penchant for baked goods and puddings. A minor mage.

Mary Hobbs: Thirty-four years old. Curly blonde hair which she keeps braided most of the time and blue eyes.

Pumpkin: Newborn Child. Dark hair and eyes.

Lord Otar, King of the Owls, and Watcher of the Woods: Larger than most owls. White owl with black face, legs, and wing tips. Golden-colored eyes. He and his mate Tifa are immortal creatures created by a High Guardian to help watch over those in Angland. They both have magic.

Purple Magic

Part 2

The Invitation

"Pay more attention, Pumpkin!" Granny Hobbs scolded when the tree the boy was supposed to defend himself from did not explode.

"By now, you should know I will not harm what does me no harm, Granny," Pumpkin declared.

"In two days, you will become visible to the world, boy, and so will your magic. You must learn to defend yourself, or you will die."

Pumpkin looked around and spied a stump left behind by a woodcutter. He used his mind to create a spell, then watched the stump explode into pieces no bigger than a toothpick.

The shield spell Granny had cast earlier, protected them from the storm of wood chips that came flying their way.

Granny Hobbs smiled. The boy was gifted with magic far superior to any she had ever known. When he put his mind to it, he could wreak havoc. The problem was he rarely was in the mood to do so. She looked at him with both pride and sadness. Despite all she could do, he undoubtedly, would not live out the week. Her eyes grew moist at that thought.

Pumpkin sensed her grief. He accepted his fate more so than his mother and great-grandmother. He reached out and patted her on the shoulder to comfort her. "I need to go gather the flock, Granny. I am sure the noise of that tree exploding has scattered them."

"While you do that, I will go help your mother finish harvesting what we can from the garden. As cold as the air is today, it will frost the plants by morning."

Pumpkin turned and made his way down the trail that led to the meadow below. He could see that most of the sheep had fled into the woods. His eyes rounded when he saw the missing sheep come running out of the woods bleating noisily. He ran down the hill, ready to defend the animals from whatever was chasing them but stopped when he saw Otar come flying out of the trees.

"Thank you for gathering the sheep," he said as the owl landed nearby on a dead limb of a fallen tree.

"Not my doing. Tifa is the one watching over your flock while you practice magic. I am here on a more serious matter."

"Then thank her for me," Pumpkin said.

"She will join us once she finds all the strays," the owl said gruffly. "You can praise her when she does."

Pumpkin nodded and then waited for the Lord of the Woods to speak. He did not need to ask why the owl was here. Granny had burned that into his brain. He faced certain death in two days' time.

"Your progress is remarkable for one who is still a human fledgling. Your magic is strong, but—"

"But not strong enough," Pumpkin interrupted, looking up at the owl, a frown on his face. "Granny has told me the same."

The owl ruffled his feathers in agitation. He knew Pumpkin was a victim of magic forces he knew nothing about, and that irritated him.

"Now that you have accepted your fate, we can work to change it."

"Change it?" Pumpkin questioned, his mouth dropping open.

"Yes. While you have only learned about your magic this past year, I have known about it before you were born. The ancient one, who lives in a cave high above this meadow, called me to witness your birth. She has taken an interest in you." Otar knew why the Dragon Queen watched the boy, but he also knew it was not his place to tell the Pumpkin the truth.

"What's her name?"

"Queen Azura. She is the last of the dragons in Angland."

"A dragon? Like those in the storybooks that Granny has?"

"I have not seen the books, so I cannot answer that question. Azura has silver and gold scales that sparkle like the stars. Her horns are silver, and so are her eyes. She has lots of teeth as well, but do not be frightened. She will not harm you. Just know that when she spreads her wings, they are so large that they black out the sunlight. Though she rarely flies during the day. She avoids contact with mankind. Most have forgotten about her.

"Doesn't she get lonely? I would."

"We owls visit her regularly, and so do the eagles. The priests of Tablea still take her food until the snow begins to fall. Then they cannot get over the mountain. She sleeps a great deal through the winter, as do most dragons. They do not like the cold weather."

"Where is Tablea?" Pumpkin asked.

"Tablea is by the great sea on the other side of those mountains," Otar replied, using his wing to point toward the mountain range with the volcano. "Few who live on this side ever go there. The journey takes a week or more to travel around and over the mountains. But enough of Tablea. It is your dilemma we need to be addressing. Put your sheep in their pens tonight. Meet me here at daylight! Wear a cloak as it will be cold in the high country. We will leave as the sun rises tomorrow. The Dragon Queen has called for you. If anyone can change your fate, it is her."

Before Pumpkin could ask more questions, Tifa flew up and lighted upon a branch. Though it was a lower limb than the one Otar perched on, their heads were equal in height, as she was a bit larger than her mate.

Pumpkin stood and bowed. "Thank you, Lady Tifa, for finding my lost sheep."

"You are most welcome, Pumpkin," Tifa said. Unlike Otar's gravelly voice, her words were soft, like velvet.

Pumpkin gave her a grateful smile.

"Meet us here at daylight!" Otar commanded as he prepared to take flight.

"I have calmed your sheep with magic," Tifa said as Otar took to the air. "You will have no problem getting them into the pens tonight. I think they have had enough adventure for today."

Pumpkin thanked Tifa with a bow, then watched her fly off.

Character

Lady Tifa, Queen of the Owls: Silver-blue in color with dark blue speckles. Sparkling emerald-green eyes light up her dark blue face.

Purple Magic

Part 3

Off to See the Dragon

Mary's spinning wheel was kept in an alcove adjacent to the kitchen. She sat at it spinning wool. She had been there most of the night, knowing her son was going into a dragon's lair. But this was not her first night to lose sleep over the fate of her son. Lord Otar's spell would end on Pumpkin's birthday which was today. She hastily wiped the tears from her eyes with the skirt of her apron before Granny saw them.

Granny was busy stirring a pan of honey butter sauce and did not see the look of grief on Mary's face. Her face was as calm as a summer day. She had used a calming spell to make sure it stayed that way.

Pumpkin had dressed in his best shirt and pants and brushed his dark curls. He cleaned his boots with a rag before he put them on. Satisfied he had done his best to look presentable, he headed for the kitchen.

Mary's face lit up with love as her son walked in, and she rose to fix his plate.

"Morning, Mother. Granny," Pumpkin greeted as he sat down at the table.

"You fix his tea, Mary. I will take him his plate," Granny said as she spooned honey butter sauce over two biscuits.

Mary fetched a cup and filled it from the kettle. As she sat it before her son, she saw his young face smiling at her, and tears threatened to spill from her eyes. She turned and went over to stand before the pantry cupboard. She quickly wiped her eyes dry with the corner of her apron before taking a small leather pouch from the pantry cupboard.

She filled the bag with food and then set it down in front of Pumpkin. "Granny put some mutton jerky, biscuits, cheese, and an apple in this bag for you to eat when you get hungry,"

"I had forgotten about lunch," Pumpkin admitted as he tied the pouch to one of his belt loops.

"I would forget about food, too, if I knew I was off to see a dragon," Granny said with a chuckle. "But I have always wanted to meet one."

Mary feared dragons, and her face lost color at Granny's words, but neither Pumpkin nor Granny noticed. Her son was busy eating his biscuits, and her grandmother was removing a pan of apple tarts from the oven.

Granny turned to set the hot pan down, then smiled and shook her head when she saw the bowls of biscuits covering the top of her baking table. Like Mary, she was having trouble sleeping, but unlike her granddaughter, who spun wool when worried, she baked when she was troubled.

Mary called Pumpkin back as he opened the kitchen door. You need to wear this today," she said as she handed him the dark wool cape she had bought for his birthday. "The hood will help keep your head warm."

Pumpkin's face lit up as he saw her gift. He thanked his mother as he slung it over his shoulders and pulled the hood over his head. He stood still as his mother buckled the cape around his neck. When she gave him a quick hug, he grinned at her, then turned and went out the door.

The mist hung thick and heavy as Pumpkin stepped out the door. He could barely see his hand in front of him, but the sheep had worn a path as wide as a road in the hillside, and he had no problem finding his way.

As he topped the hill, Pumpkin heard Otar's gravelly hoot from the valley below. He followed the trail down the backside of the hill to where the owls waited. Much to his surprise, he saw a white horse with wings standing by the tree the owls had perched while they waited for him.

"This is Fiolin," Otar said. "He comes from an afar land where dragons still live, and horses fly. He has agreed to carry you to Azura's home.

Pumpkin closed his mouth, unfroze his tongue, and immediately bowed toward the horse. "Thank you, Lord Fiolin."

"I like the way you think. But I am not a lord, Pumpkin. Call me Fi," the horse said as he moved to stand by a stump. "If you climb up on what is left of this tree, I think you will be able to reach my back. I could lift you by magic, but I have found with humans that it is best if they find their own way up instead of worrying about me dropping them on their heads."

When Fiolin was young colt, a mage practicing magic had dropped Fiolin on his head. It had not only hurt, but it had also humiliated him in front of his family and friends. He never forgot that day and was skittish about anyone being dropped on their head.

Pumpkin jumped up on the stump and pulled himself up on the horse's back. He sat up and let out a breath of relief that all had gone well.

"Just so you know, I can hear your thoughts," Fiolin said. "You are right that you cannot sit where you are due to being in the way of my wings. You need to lay flat on my back. When you are comfortable, I will use magic to bind you. Do not worry. You will not fall off. And yes, you can move your head from side to side. Use your arms to hold on to my mane. It will help with air sickness."

Pumpkin did as he was told.

"We are ready when you are, Otar," Fiolin announced once he had secured the boy to his back.

"Then we best be on our way. Use your magic to keep yourself and the boy warm, Fi. The air will turn icy long before we reach the mountain," the owl warned.

Pumpkin made a small noise of surprise and closed his eyes as the horse took to the air. When he opened them again, he found they were traveling through the mist. He pulled his hood closer as a gust of wind tried to scour him off Fiolin's back.

"The Wind, she bows before no one," Fiolin told Pumpkin, using his telepathic abilities. "She reigns supreme whether it be in the heart of a volcano, the ice fields of the northern plains, or the on the great seas that separate one land from another. Air or ground makes no difference to her. The best we can do is fly with her currents or seek shelter if she decides to storm. While you may call upon her for help using magic, do not ever think for one moment you are her master. Always remember to thank her, or she may drop you on your head."

"Thank you. I will be sure to remember that," Pumpkin called out, relaxing a bit, and beginning to enjoy the ride as he felt the warmth of Fi's body beneath him.

Note
Fiolin is one of the immortal flying horses of ancient creation that lives in another realm where most of the dragons have gone. White in color with dark eyes. Dragon Queen Esmera summoned him to bring Pumpkin to her palace, not wanting the boy to know who she is before he meets her.

Purple Magic
Part 4

Grandmother?

Dragon Queen Azura lives in a large cavern made by a volcano and later enhanced and reinforced with magic. A tempered metal grate lies over a huge fire pit that reaches down to the Magna flow beneath the earth's crust and heats the enormous stone rooms. The luminous checkered tiles on the floor were created by a fire spirit living in the volcano, using pyroclastic volcano ash and magic. Their reflective surface makes a deep red circle from the fire pit that fades into slivers of silver light, forming a giant compass star. Huge fairy lanterns powered by large fairy stone crystals, hang on iron chains, and fill the cavern with light.

Two colorful rugs made in Tablea were spread on the floor for the horse and the boy to use. An ancient wooden stand made from the limb of a *yoak tree* with a perch for the owls was brought in and set next to the rug Pumpkin would use.

Azura greeted her guests as they perched, sat, or in Fiolin's case, stood. She then made herself comfortable on a thick dragon-sized carpet.

"Before we speak of why I summoned Pumpkin here, we all must have something to eat and drink while you warm yourselves. Winter approaches and the air is cold."

Pumpkin watched as two men in gray robes with a black waist cord came in. One was carrying a tray with glasses and bowls. The other man had a basket of tarts in one hand and a basket of seeded sunflowers and clover grass. He could not help but smile as a third man appeared with a large bowl atop his hooded head and two glass pitchers of water on a tray. He was surprised to see humans living with the dragon. He watched the man with the pitchers gently set them on a table. He then took the bowl off his head and laid it in front of Fiolin. One of the other servants grabbed a pitcher and filled the bowl. The owls got the sunflowers while he got a mug of water and two berry tarts.

One of the servants set the basket with the remaining tarts in front of Azura's stool. That was when Pumpkin noticed a giant gold-colored bowl filled with water had appeared by the dragon. *Now that's magic*, he told himself.

As the boy watched the men leave, he wondered if they were slaves.

"They are not slaves, youngling. They are priests who volunteer to come and serve me. In return, I allow them to copy the ancient books that I own." She did not add that she also gave them gold to help the monastery pay for food and other things the priests needed to survive.

Pumpkin's face flamed in embarrassment. "Sorry, your Majesty, I meant no insult."

"There is no need for apology. I was explaining the why of what you were wondering about," Azura said, giving the young man a wide toothy smile.

Pumpkin's eye rounded, and he swallowed nervously as he saw her sharp teeth. Some were as long as he was tall.

"Have no fear of me, child. I would never harm you. We are family."

Fiolin's ears went up at that remark.

Otar and Tifa were not surprised. They had known from the day Pumpkin was born who had fathered him. They also knew why those memories had been wiped from his mother's and grandmother's memory and all those who lived in the kingdom of Angland and the rest of the world.

"Family?" Pumpkin questioned as he struggled to swallow the piece of tart he had in his mouth.

"Yes. Your father was my human son."

"Was?" Pumpkin cried out, tears gathering in his eyes as he realized his father was dead. Granny had always told him she did not know how he came to be. "*You were born. That's all your mother, and I know,*" she had said.

"Yes, his name was Hawk. He was murdered a week before you were born. He was poisoned. That is why I cast a spell across the land and wiped the memories of his existence from the land. No one could know you were my grandson. They would have killed not only you but also your mother and great-grandmother to keep your birth a secret. I know now that I should have brought you to live here with me, but I was so aggrieved. All I could think of was keeping your birth a secret. With Otar's and Tifa's help, I achieved that."

"Am I going to turn into a dragon?" Pumpkin cut in.

"No. Of course not." Azura answered. "You are human, as was your father. A dragon can take human shape if desired, which I did when I was Queen of Angland. However, any children born will never be dragons, but they are a dragon child and have dragon magic, as do you. Your father was a king. My other child, Bertrice, is the Queen. I am sure you have heard of her."

Pumpkin nodded. Granny and his Mother told him, often enough, he was to hide if he saw the Queen.

Fiolin was just as impressed by her words as Pumpkin was. He looked over at the boy. "You are a prince by birth and a dragon by heart. Like your father, you will grow up to be a mighty mage."

"No. I don't think so," Pumpkin said, shaking his head with sadness in his eyes. "Tomorrow is All Hallows' Eve in our land. It is the day I become visible in my world. And the day I die."

Fiolin glared at the dragon.

Otar and Tifa kept their eyes on Azura. They had yet to learn how she would save the boy, but they trusted her with his life and their own when it came down to it.

"You will not die, Pumpkin. That is why I had Otar bring you here. It is time for your dragon-self to rise."

Before he could ask what, she meant by that statement, a golden halo of light enveloped Pumpkin, and he began to rise. His dark eyes glowed like warm magma as he hung in the air, and all the knowledge and magic of the dragons filled his mind and body.

He stayed that way for some minutes, then slowly descended until his feet touched the rug beneath his feet. His eyes quit glowing and closed as darkness claimed him.

As he started to fall, Azura caught him with a spell, and laid him gently on the rug.

Fiolin snorted again.

"Do not worry, Fiolin. The boy's body needs to sleep while his mind works on the magic he has been given. Normally, it takes years to teach someone what he has learned today. He will wake within the hour and be ravenous. This basket of quilaberry tarts is for him. Once he has eaten and drank his fill, we will go up to the top of the mountain and test his skills. If all goes well, it should be a memorable day. In the meantime, I suggest you drink the water in your bowl. It is from the magic spring beneath this cavern. It will cure all that ails you and bring youth back to your body. The clover is fresh, sweet, and from Tablea."

Character

Dragon Queen Azura Morningstar: Her scales are silver and gold in color and sparkle as light hits them. Her horns are silver, and so are her eyes.

Purple Magic

Part 5

I Know My Name

Pumpkin returned home with the excitement of a child with good news to tell, and all the knowledge and magic of dragon kind. He ran to his mother and embraced her as he whispered, "My name is Pumpkin Greystone. My Father was King Hawk." He then did the same for his great-grandmother. Both women reacted differently to the sudden rush of lost memories that filled their minds.

Mary sat down at the table, her mind shattered as she found she was wedded and a widow in the same moment. Tears ran down her face as her beloved's face filled her mind.

Granny's face turned red as she remembered the wedding of Mary and Hawk. "Who did this to us? Who took away our memories?" she questioned angrily. "All these years, I have lived with the sorrow of believing my granddaughter had been violated by one with magic." She started to rise from the table.

"I will tell you all I know, Granny" Pumpkin said, motioning for her to sit down as he went and patted his mother's shoulder.

"I am sorry, Mother. But there is much to tell, and our time is short. Grandmother will come for me. We need to be in the pumpkin patch before the midnight hour."

"No! I cannot lose you too!" Mary cried as she rose from her chair, grabbed Pumpkin's hand, and pulled him toward the door. "We need to find a place to hide."

"We could hide in the root cellar. It is beneath the ground. It may hide Pumpkin's magic long enough for us to figure out what to do. I may not have the magic Otar has, but I do know a good invisibility spell," Granny said as she started to rise from her chair again.

"I will not be hiding in the root cellar, Granny," Pumpkin said, refusing to budge another step. "Not tonight. But you and Mother will take shelter there until I return. That is part of what I need to tell you. Now, if you both will sit down, I will tell you the rest of the story."

Granny's mouth dropped open with surprise at his words and the tone of his voice, but nevertheless, she sat back down.

Once his mother returned to her chair, Pumpkin told them all about Azura, the memory spell, how his father had died, and the gift of purple magic he had received from the stars was dragon magic.

"The plan is for you and Mother to take refuge in the cellar, Granny. I will then cast a spell that will make the house, barn and sheep pens invisible. Grandmother says that most demons and warlocks will burn the house should they take an interest in it. All anyone will see when they pass by the farm is a thorn thicket."

"And what will you be doing while we are in the cellar?" Granny asked.

"I will be with Grandmother exposing those who killed my Father," Pumpkin answered grimly.

Purple Magic

Part 6

Birthplace

Pumpkin looked at the field of tall brown grass that now covered the pumpkin patch where he had been born. He saw several saplings scattered across the land and knew it had been years since anyone had grown pumpkins here. He wondered why the farmer no longer worked his land.

Azura flipped her tail, and the field filled with pumpkins as far as one could see.

"Thank you, Grandmother."

"You are welcome. This is what I saw the day you were born. Of course, my pumpkins are dragon size, but they do bring color to what was a bleak landscape. Now I only need to add a fire pit to keep you warm."

Pumpkin ducked his head as dry wood came flying from the woods and landed in a pile in front of him.

"I should have warned you," Azura apologized. "Come stand here by me, as there is more to come!"

Pumpkin moved to her side and watched as his grandmother brought rocks from a creek behind them to make a ring around the wood.

Satisfied with her work, the dragon blew a breath of flames, and the wood caught fire.

Pumpkin used his magic to move one of the giant squashes over to the fire pit and sat down on it to warm himself while they waited for him to become visible to the world.

The boy needed no watch to tell him the midnight hour was upon them. A ripple of light washed over him as Otar's protective spell ended.

"It will not be long now," Azura told him. "The ghosts will come first as they are free to roam on All Hallows' Eve. They are attracted to magic as moths to flames. Do not fear them. They cannot harm you."

"What are ghosts?" Pumpkin asked, not familiar with the word.

"They are the souls of humans, who for one reason or another get trapped in this world instead of ascending as most do."

"Granny calls them spirits. And they can harm you. Mother said mist spirits killed her mother and father."

"Yes, that is the name for them in this land. Your grandparents were killed by demons who walk around in shadow form. Humans believe they are spirits. Never make that mistake. A true ghost is a pale silver color, or blue. Demons or cursed ones are always dark in color."

"What is a cursed one?"

"One that committed the foulest deeds while living and is doomed to haunt the spot where they died for eternity," Azura answered. "While cursed ones cannot harm others, it can be frightening or annoying for those who can hear their cries. Thankfully, few who can hear them, and getting fewer every year as magic is slowly disappearing from this land."

"Why is that?"

"Dragons bring magic to their world. I am the last of my kind in Angland."

"What happened to all the other dragons?" Pumpkin asked.

"By the time magic became dark in this land, only a few dragons continued to live here. Even my brother Baldigar went to live in Asterland with the fairies. Eventually, I was the only one who stayed in Angland. But enough of reliving the past," Azura said as memories of her family and friends assaulted her mind. "Right now, it is the future that we need to be concerned with."

When Pumpkin remained silent, Azura continued. "Next will come the demons. They are also attracted by magic because they feed on it. They are dangerous. However, most will not attack when they realize you are more powerful than they are. Leave those that do to me. I will fry them into crisps.

"For now, I will speak only with my mind, so that only you can hear me. Remember, they cannot see me, and the magic will appear to be your own. Word of one possessing dragon magic will travel fast. Within the hour, we can expect several warlocks and witches to come and investigate. Do not worry. None can harm you no matter dangerous they appear to be."

Pumpkin got to his feet as he saw several silver lights coming his way. "Those must be ghosts," he said.

"Yes," Azura confirmed. "Leave them be. They will leave once the demons begin to arrive. Which reminds me, I have yet to put up my ward shield."

Pumpkin watched as a dome of magic with silver sparkles surrounded them. The boy did not realize he was sitting in the middle of a dragon fire shield.

A few minutes later, two demons arrived. Both were dark green, ugly, and had boar-like snouts and tusks. One reached out to claw the delicious-looking man-child. When his hand hit the magic shield, he shrieked in pain and jerked his hand back.

The other demon with him stepped back to take a better look. He sniffed the air, but all he could smell was the burnt flesh of his brother.

Several more demons attracted by Pumpkin's magic arrived. None of them approached the boy, but they eyed the injured one with hungry eyes.

Within a few minutes, dozens of demons in all different forms and sizes stood around the fire pit. Many drooled as they sensed the fountain of magic within the boy. Little did they realize a dragon stood behind the boy.

Jars and Lars, two purple-skinned demon brothers that stood more than seven feet tall with goat-like horns and faces, kicked several of the smaller demons out of their way as they moved closer to the source of the magic.

However, they did not attack the shield. Instead, each picked up a pumpkin and tossed it at the shield to test its strength. Much to their dismay, the pumpkins bounced off the shield and flew back toward those who had thrown them, striking them in the face.

The other demons howled with laughter as the pumpkins exploded and plastered orange pulp and slimy seeds all over the two arrogant brothers.

Pumpkin wanted to laugh but instinctively knew it would weaken his position. He clamped his jaws shut and kept the glare on his face.

"Did no one ever tell you, braggarts, not to throw food at a ward shield?" a new voice asked as King Trent Daregard appeared at the edge of the field. "Even a newborn poltergeist knows better. Food will rebound and... Well, there's no need for me to say more. The pumpkin cooking on your horns and running down your faces tells the story," Trent said, a grin on his handsome face.

More howls of laughter filled the night air.

Jars growled, angry that the mage dared mock him, but he did not attack the man. He knew Trent's magic was more powerful than his.

Trent turned and eyed the throng of demons with distaste. "I suggest you all clear out. That boy is royal business. The Queen will be here shortly, and as you all know, she has no patience for your kind."

The demons hurried off. If the queen was coming, so were her guards, but they only went as far as the woods, hiding among the trees. The queen and her warlocks would kill the boy, but not without a fight. There would be the dead and dying left for them to feed on what magic was left in them, not to mention filling their bellies with what flesh was left.

The largest of the demons—Roc—stayed. He was a volcano demon and not afraid of fire. Heat could not harm him.

Jars and Lars stopped to watch when they saw Roc head for the boy and began tearing at the fire shield.

Azura knew the invisible flames of the shield would not stop the behemoth, but she also knew that ice would. She blew a breath of frozen air at him, using a dragon spell to make it colder. She watched him freeze where he stood. She then blew a concussive blast of air his way and the volcano demon crumbled into a heap of red ice.

Jars and Lars looked at what was left of Roc, then at each other, and without a word, both turned and ran.

Trent's eyes narrowed. He knew dragon magic when he saw it. "Who are you?" he asked the boy.

"When the Queen gets here, I will introduce myself, but not before then," Pumpkin replied.

Trent used magic to contact Bertrice and told her she needed to come. The boy with dragon magic had asked for her. He knew it would not be long before she arrived.

As he studied the lad, he was surprised to find that he longed to weep. "You interest me, boy. I sense I know who you are, but I am unable to figure out why," he said before he went to sit on a pumpkin at the edge of the field to wait for his lady.

Character

Consort King Trent Daregard: A Wizard Mage married to Queen Bertrice. A tall, handsome man with brown hair and eyes. Sixty-two years of age, but for a Wizard Mage that is young as they generally live several thousand years.

Purple Magic
Part 7

Death by Kablitz

*"**He thinks he** knows me,"* Pumpkin told Azura, using his telepathic abilities.

"Yes, Either the spell I put up twelve years ago is starting to fade or..." Azura stopped there unwilling to reveal more. They needed to wait until they found the murderers before discussing Trent with Pumpkin. "What we need to learn is if he can he be trusted? For that, we will have to wait and see."

The pumpkin patch lit up as Queen Bertrice and four of her ministers appeared before the shield that guarded Pumpkin. Within a few seconds, another light disturbed the darkness as the eldest of the mages, Gunter and Jevel, each ferrying a palace guard and a handmaiden, made their appearance.

Small bursts of light filled the night as dozens of mages and witches around the kingdom, summoned by the queen, arrived.

The queen spoke to Trent, then approached the fire pit where Pumpkin stood behind the shield.

Three of her ministers followed her. Nardu hesitated as he sensed what kind of magic they were facing. "My Queen!" he called out. As Bertrice turned around to glare at him, he added, "The boy has dragon magic."

Bertrice nodded then turned to look at the boy who stared back at her. "Who are you!" she commanded.

"I am Pumpkin Greystone, son of King Hawk Greystone, your Majesty," Pumpkin said, bowing to show respect. He did not realize his name was the key to finding those who killed his father.

Light washed over the land as Azura's memory spell was broken. There were murmurs of shock and despair as all those present remembered the death of their beloved king.

"You are Hawk's son?" Bertrice asked, tears running down her face as she remembered and mourned her brother's death. She used her magic to wash them away. This was not the time to show weakness. She needed to find out what had happened.

"Why did you kill my father?" Pumpkin accused, his eyes turning to flames as he spoke.

Bertrice's eyes rounded with surprise. "Why would I kill Hawk? I loved him. He was my brother."

Pumpkin was shaken by her words but kept his mouth shut. "*Why did you not tell me that, Grandmother?*" he asked.

"*I am truly sorry, Pumpkin. It had to be this way if I am to discover who killed your father,*" Azura replied. "*Ask her if he was a threat to her throne?*"

"Perhaps to keep your throne," Pumpkin replied.

"No. You are wrong, child. Your father was King, and I the Queen. We shared the throne equally," Bertrice explained patiently, knowing the boy had no memory of what Hawk had meant to her.

Azura let out a loud roar as she ended her invisibility spell. "You poisoned my son!" she thundered as she appeared behind her grandson, making all those in the pumpkin patch and those in the woods quake with fear.

Ministers Eidel and Rujon both tried to cast a travel spell but found they had no magic. Azura had used a spell to remove it. They turned and ran.

Bertrice turned around to look for the ones her mother had accused. When she saw her two ministers running away, she cast a spell and dragged them back. She then cast a truth spell. "Did you poison Hawk?" she asked, her eyes turning to flames.

"Rujon did it! He killed the King," Eidel cried out.

Bertrice froze the two men where they stood. "No one is to leave, Trent!" she commanded before she turned and walked unharmed through the dragon shield.

"Mother," she greeted as she looked up at Azura. "Why would you believe I killed Hawk?"

"I did not think you killed him, Bertrice, but I knew someone at the palace had. They protected themselves by casting a spell to hide their guilt. Tonight, that spell was broken by Pumpkin's presence once he stated his name as he is of the same blood as his father, and that blood is on their hands. If you use your dragon senses, you can see it. When I entered their minds, I found them that murdered your brother."

"Why did they kill him?" Bertrice asked, turning to look at the two men. She used her dragon vision and saw what her mother saw. Her ministers' hands were indeed covered with blood. She then looked at the hands of her other ministers, advisors, guards, and those gathered to be sure there were no others involved in her brother's death.

"From their minds, I have discovered Hawk found them stealing gold from the treasury. When he turned to call for the guards to come and take them to the dungeon, Rujon used a poison dart to stop him. Eidel then cast an invisibility spell. The two of them carried Hawk to his bed chamber, leaving him to die," Azura answered emotionally.

Bertrice's eyes lit up with flames as she walked back through the shield. She used her magic to lift the men off the ground. When they stood before her, she pronounced their sentence.

"These murderers of my brother King Hawk are to be carried into the woods, tied to trees, and left there for the demons." Bertrice pronounced. "The punishment is Kablitz!" she commanded, her voice echoing across the field and into the woods. "King Trent, Minister Gunter, and Minister Jevel will witness the ritual. Death to any demon who dares to take more than a nibble. Sate your hunger elsewhere tonight!"

"What is Kablitz?" Pumpkin asked Azura.

"Death by nibbling. A fitting sentence for the murderers of a dragon child," she replied.

Pumpkin nodded, but at the same time, the thought of the two men being eaten, nibble by nibble, while still alive made his stomach roll.

Azura sensed his thoughts but did not defend her daughter's sentence. The traitors' death by Kablitz would spread across the land. Bertrice, Pumpkin, and his family would be safer for it.

Perhaps next All Hallows' Eve, we can gather here for a festival to celebrate Pumpkin's birth. It is long overdue, she told herself.

Character

Queen Bertrice Greystone: A beautiful woman with long dark wavy hair and dark eyes. She has ruled Angland for the past sixty years. As a dragon child, she is immortal and does not age past her twenty-fifth year.

The Prouter Curse
Manhattan 2020

The Fireman

He struggled to get out outside. His face mask was sooty, his clothing was scorched, and smoke curled up into the air from his shoes. He jumped through the flames that covered the door, and once outside, pulled the mask off and gasped for air.

"From what I see, you should have died in there, but then you never could do anything right," stated the man dressed in black, standing there waiting for him.

"Thanks, Uncle. I love you too," Danner countered with a grin which he knew would make his uncle grit his teeth.

Abbelton Prouter watched with a frown of impatience on his face as his nephew took a gray cat out of his coat pocket and set it on the ground. The cat without hesitation, scurried off, jumping over fire hoses to get to the alley. Then darted past the firemen spraying water on the burning house.

"You told me you would come stay at the house with the rest of the family tonight, yet I find you here risking your life to save a cat."

"I was on my way when the call came in for this apartment building. As for saving others that is what I do. I am a fireman," Danner said, not saying a word about the two children he had already brought out of the building.

"Maybe so, but today is Halloween. I have told you what happens tonight. One of us will be taken by the Master Wizard in payment of a debt incurred hundreds of years ago by Josiah Prouter."

"Well, I think it is time to tell him the debt has been paid ten times over, and he needs to make a new deal with someone else."

"I cannot speak to the High Wizard that way, you fool. He would strike me dead."

Danner shrugged. "So, what have you got to lose. He is going to take one of you anyway."

Abbelton's face flushed red at the lack of respect from his nephew. "You are in just as much danger as the rest of us are," he said through gritted teeth.

"So you tell me, but my mother is dead now, so he won't be taking her. As for my father, no worries there, he is not a Prouter."

Abbelton found himself irritated at Danner's attitude, and he all but shouted, "It is not you that I am worried about, it is your cousins."

The grin disappeared off Danner's face. He liked his younger cousins, his aunt, and his uncle for that matter, but he rarely let anyone see that side of him. It was easier to pretend indifference than it was to let them know he cared. For they all exhibited more regard for Albert, Uncle Abbelton's elderly valet, than they did for him. Except Juneth, she always asked if he would help her with her homework or to play songs on the piano and sing with her.

"Let me go tell my Captain that I am leaving. But know this, Uncle, since you will not tell the High Wizard to suck it up, I am going to. If he strikes me dead, then you will be rid of me for good."

Abbelton watched his nephew walk off. He was not happy at the thought of losing his nephew, but a glimmer of hope broke into the darkness of his despair. For if Danner did as he said, he would probably be the one taken, if only for punishment, thus leaving his children to live out most of their lives before the High Wizard returned.

* * *

I need to know all about this wizard guy, and what deal was struck, if I am going to argue my case," Danner said, as his uncle drove them across town to the family mansion.

Abbelton made a face. He did not like to talk about the family secret. "The High Wizard is head of the Society of Ancient Mages," he began.

"Mages? You mean, like magic people?"

"Yes. I have magic, and so do you, but somehow, you have managed to suppress that trait."

Danner did not reply. He did not want his uncle to know that he had been using what he called kinetic energy to get in and out of burning buildings. He had always thought the energy came from his Father, but he now realized it could be from his Mother's side.

"What you need to know is that he is the most powerful wizard ever born, and according to what I have heard, he is more than a thousand years old," Abbelton continued.

"What happens to those he takes?"

"They become his servants."

"Even if they don't want the job?"

"Yes. Once he casts his spell of servitude, you will have no problem doing whatever he tells you to do."

"Nothing like a magical lobotomy, I always say," Danner muttered.

"Is nothing sacred to you?" Abbelton snapped.

"Yes, the freedom to choose where I go or do not go. But never mind that, tell me why your great, great, great, whatever, bargained or sold off Prouters that were not yet born?"

Abbelton heaved a worried sigh before he answered the question. "When Josiah Prouter landed in America, he saw land for the taking, and promptly grabbed several hundred acres of what is now, Manhattan Island, and New York City."

Danner whistled. "Two hundred acres. I did not realize you owned that much land."

"I don't. Over the years, property has been sold off or claimed by various governments for public use. Now we are down to about a half dozen acres here in New York, and a half dozen or so holdings on the Island."

"Anyway, getting back to Josiah Prouter," Abbelton said. "He used what gold he had left to build a dock for those who came to trade, and had buildings built which he rented out to merchants for shops. He did quite well until someone else decided they wanted what he had. When he would not sell out cheap, they burned his buildings, and in general wreaked havoc among his tenants until most fled the premises. Realizing he was about to lose all he worked for, he asked the High Wizard for help. The price was one Prouter every fifty years."

Danner shook his head. "An agreement is binding only to those who agree to it."

"In the world of magic, an agreement can include those yet to be born," Abbelton said.

"What about an expiration date? Surely, there has to be something about that," Danner argued.

"I know nothing about that," Abbelton admitted. "Everything I know about the High Wizard comes from listening to conversations by other mages when I attend the annual gatherings. I never ask questions about him for fear of bringing myself to his attention as he sends several of his red-robe apprentices to the gatherings. To tell you the truth, I am not very good at magic, and rarely practice it."

"What color robes do the wizards normally wear?"

"White of course. We don't practice dark magic. The dark wizards that wear black robes don't bother us, and we don't bother them."

"Do you have a copy of the agreement? I need to look at it," Danner asked, changing the subject.

Abbelton shook his head. "If there is such a thing, I have no knowledge of it. All I know is what my father told me fifty years ago when my brother disappeared. He never talked about it again, nor would allow anyone to mention Bastion's name. Or at least, not in front of him. I did ask my Mother when he was not around, but she just shook her head and started to cry. Needless to say, I never asked her about him again."

"You were six years old, fifty years ago. How old was your brother?"

"Eleven. I remember that because we had just celebrated his birthday."

"My mother would have been three or four at the time. Did she forget about him?" Danner asked. "Because I don't recall her ever saying a word about having another brother."

"For a time, she would ask me, or Mother where was Baba? That was what she called him. But even at the age of four, she understood she was not to ask Father," Abbelton replied.

"Do you think Uncle Bastion will come with the High Wizard tonight?"

Abbelton was glad it was dark because that question made a lump in his throat. He cleared his throat before he answered. "I don't know who will come or how it is done. I only know that someone will come. Just before he died, Father wrote the date on two pieces of paper, and then gave one to me, and left one to be given to your mother when she was found.

Danner's mind flashed back to the day he had cleaned out his mother's desk. He had unlocked the top drawer and had been surprised to see there was only one piece of paper inside with a date on it—today's date, he thought—and the words Halloween Day. Nothing else. He had wondered at the time, why she bothered to lock the drawer. Now he knew.

* * *

Fifteen-year old Rosie met them at the door, and threw her arms around Danner, clinging to him tearfully. "You should not have come Danner. I don't want to lose you," she said.

"I don't want to lose you either, Rosie," Danner declared.

Rosie's dark head reared back. "What do you mean?" she asked, her blue eyes wide with alarm.

Danner looked over Rosie's head at his uncle. "Does he only take male members of the family?" he asked.

Abbelton shook his head.

"Then why have you not told her that?"

By this time, Rosie had turned her head to look at her father. She did not need to ask him whether she was at risk at being snatched by the dark wizard he claimed was coming tonight, the tears in his eyes told her more than she wanted to know. She let go of Danner, took a deep breath, and blew it out noisily. "Well, I think I will go sit with Mother and Juneth. They might need me," she said calmly.

As she walked away, Danner heard her mutter, "This family is freaking insane. Daddy just sold one of us to the dark side, and no one seems upset about it but me." He felt sorry for her, but he dared not tell her that, as he knew it would melt the mental glue that was holding her together.

Abbelton's face blanched as he heard her words. He realized no matter which one them got picked, if it was not him, the others would never forgive him. And Danner was right about trying to fight it. He had had years to work on finding a way to end the contract, but it had never occurred to him to do such a thing. *Why?* he asked himself. *Why did I not think to fight back?*

He cried out as darkness claimed his vision. *"There is no fighting back for Prouters. I will always be waiting for the next one. The contract is not over until I say it is,"* said a voice so cold it made him shiver as it spoke to his mind.

Abbelton felt a wave of dizziness wash over him as the darkness receded, and light filled the hallway. He reached out and put a hand on the wall to help support his shaky legs.

Danner turned back to see what was wrong. When he saw his uncle's face turn the color of color of fresh concrete. He moved toward him. "You all right?" he asked.

"No," Abbelton croaked. He then cleared his throat before he added, "Help me get to the day room. He will be here soon. He just spoke to me."

"What did he say"

"The contract is not over until he says it is," Abbelton murmured.

Danner's brow went up as it occurred to him that if the wizard was trying to squelch the rebellion before he got here, there might yet be a way to stop him.

Lyda gave a cry when she saw Danner holding Abbelton up as they entered the room.

"Go find Albert, Christoff! Tell him to bring your father's heart medicine, and a glass of water."

"You are on heart medicine?" Danner asked as he helped his uncle his into his chair.

Abbelton nodded, not wanting others to hear him admit he was ill.

"You never told me. I am sorry that I made you angry tonight. I would not have teased you, had I known."

Abbelton shook his head. "This is not your fault, Danner," he whispered.

"No, it is not. But it is not your fault either, though, I was quick to blame you."

"As was I," Rosie said as she knelt to take her father's boots off and put on his slippers.

"And I," Lyda admitted as she reached for the glass of water Christoff had brought from the kitchen. "I am sorry, dear, I should have realized the stress you have been under."

Abbelton did not speak. He was afraid he would start weeping if he tried to say one word to console them.

Albert rushed in with the medicine. "Should I call the doctor, Sir?" he asked.

"No!" Abbelton wheezed. "There is not time for a doctor. Just give me the medicine!"

Albert handed him a pill.

When Lyda saw his eyes were on her, she handed him the water.

"I think it would be better if we all go set down, and give uncle room to breathe," Danner said.

Albert went back to his TV show in the kitchen. Everyone else went and set down on the family-size sofa, but their eyes remained on the chair Abbelton sat in. The youngest member of the family, eleven year old Juneth, sat wiping tears from her eyes as Rosie patted her hand.

* * *

It was fifteen minutes to midnight when the room went dark, so dark you could not see your hand in front of your face, and the room's temperature dropped considerably. Rosie and Juneth cried out in fear as a ball of light lit up the room, and a figure in a red robe stepped out of it.

The lights came back on.

Danner felt a shiver of fear run down his spine as he saw the wizard's face was gray and bony, he looked more dead than alive, and his eyes appeared to be flames. No wonder everyone is scared of him, he thought swallowing nervously.

"Well, well, I see I have a nice batch of young people to choose from," the High Wizard said, his voice gravelly from age.

"I will gladly go with you," Abbelton said. "There is no need to take the children."

"No, Daddy!" Rosie cried out.

The High Wizard ignored the girl's outburst as he turned to look at Abbelton. "Why would I want you, old man. You are but a few years away from death. No, I think I will take that little witch with the blonde hair," he said, turning to point at Juneth.

Everyone in the room protested, but Juneth. She had fainted, her body slumping against Danner.

Danner gently shoved her toward Rosie, then got to his feet, letting his aunt take his place.

As Lyda held her daughter's unconscious body, she glared at the wizard. "You cannot have her!" she cried out.

"No matter what happens, stay where you are!" Danner told his aunt and cousins as he used what he called kinetic energy to make a bubble of light around him and those sitting on the sofa. It was the same light bubble he used when getting in and out of burning buildings.

"Ah, a young mage with a bit of talent, but obviously, not very smart," the High Wizard said before he cast a withering spell at Danner with a smile on his face. He expected to see the man dissolve into dust, but when nothing happened, his smile disappeared. He then cast a fire spell, but the flames died as they hit mage's light shield. He dredged up one of his dragon spells, angry enough that he did not care if he killed them all off, including the witch he had selected. He used both hands to cast the spell.

The dragon's breath spell left his hands with the force of a gale, picking up furniture and throwing it against the walls, but fizzled out to no more than a breeze as it hit the bubble shield.

Impossible! the High Wizard thought. Nothing he had ever encountered before was able to resist dragon spells.

"There are those more powerful than dragons," a voice spoke to his mind. *"Or have you lived so long in your self-created hell that you have forgotten about us, Roltarmus?"*

"You have no business here. A contract was made," the wizard replied sharply, realizing who spoke to him.

"Yes, but you terminated it a few minutes ago."

"I did not," the wizard argued, so angry he now spoke aloud.

"Check Rule number one hundred and fifty-three: clause two in the Book of Contracts. You will find that when Abbelton volunteered to be your new apprentice, and you turned him down, you officially ended the contract. So it is

now, you, who has no business here or anymore business here—ever, with those who belong to the Prouter family."

The High Wizard stood there with flames surrounding him, such was his anger. He turned to look at the young mage who had created the bubble shield. "You are not a Prouter. What are you doing here, and who are you?" he questioned, hoping to show he had been tricked.

My mother was a Prouter. My name is Danner Angelson. I am a fireman, and saving others is what I do."

A rumble of thunder filled the room as the High Wizard disappeared, leaving behind a plume of smoke, and an acrid stench of sulfur.

"*He will not be coming back,*" a voice spoke softly to Danner's mind.

"*Thanks, Dad.*"

Danner saw the carpet was on fire where the wizard had been standing and grabbed a vase of flowers off the fireplace mantle. He then tossed the flowers and threw the water on the fire.

"Chris, run and grab the fire extinguisher in the kitchen!" he commanded as he watched steamy smoke boil up out of the carpet.

"Is he gone?" Abbelton whispered.

"Yes, and according to Father, he won't be back," Danner answered, keeping his voice down so that only his uncle heard him.

Abbelton began to cry. "All these years, I thought your mom was delusional. How I wronged her.

"Mom always appreciated that you helped her escape. She told me that the day before she died."

Rosie jumped up off the couch. "What are you talking about?" she asked.

"I was talking about how disappointed I was when Danner chose to be a fireman, rather than become a Prouter employee. I was wrong. He used his fireman skills tonight and saved us all." Abbelton answered.

There was no way he was going to tell his wife and children the family secret that he had kept hidden all these years. That his sister had claimed her unborn child was fathered by an angel. His father was so angry with her, he had her committed to a sanitarium for the mentally ill. Knowing he had to do something to save her before the ambulance came to take her away, he had climbed the vine that grew on that side of the house. Then he helped her climb down the vine. It was sixteen years before he saw her again, and that was when she came back for their father's funeral. A year later she died—pancreatic cancer, the doctors said. Danner stayed with them through high school, then moved back to Jessica's house when he started college. That had been five years ago.

Danner was glad that his uncle had not mentioned his mother. He was not ashamed of her or his father, but he knew it would change how his aunt and cousins felt about him.

Before Rosie could ask more questions, Christoff appeared with the fire extinguisher. Danner grabbed it, then used it to spray the rug. When he was satisfied the fire was out, he picked up the vase, put the flowers back in it, and set it back on the fireplace mantle. The fire extinguisher he left on the floor. It might be needed again.

"Tomorrow, you need to see about getting the carpet replaced, Aunt Lyda," Danner said. "This section of the rug can smolder for days. Not only will the smell be bad, it could burst into flames again."

Lyda let go of Juneth, who had recovered from her fainting spell, and stood. She looked around at the broken furniture, drapes hanging askew, and other damage to the room. "What are we going to tell them? I mean, this is not a normal situation, is it?"

"We will simply tell them that someone broke into the house while we were out, and we came home to find this mess," Abbelton said. "I will have one of those cleaning outfits come in and remove the carpet and furniture. The painting over the fireplace and grandmother's rocking chair or anything else that you want to keep, Lyda, can be put in the music room until the work is finished. For years we have talked about redoing this room. Now is the time to get it done."

Danner found himself yawning and looked at the clock. He was surprised to see it was only a few minutes past midnight.

Lyda saw him yawn. "Why don't you sleep in your old room, Danner. We keep it ready for you. It is too late to be out traveling at this time of night."

Danner nodded and headed for the stairs. Christoff followed him.

"You were awesome, bro. That line about saving others was great. I am thinking about becoming a fireman too, like you" the boy told Danner.

Danner stopped on the landing. "Being a fireman is a good thing, Chris, but you are the last to carry on the Prouter name. You need to finish your education, then go work with your father, and learn the business to protect your own interests, and the rest of the family for that matter, which includes me. Your father probably has not said much about it to you, but Prouter Properties and investments is a billion dollar business. It takes a strong knowledgeable person to keep it running smoothly. While I am on the trustee board simply because I am a Prouter, that does not mean I have the knowledge or the ability to run the corporation. I am counting on you taking that job on when the time comes."

Christoff had hung his head in disappointment when Danner told him he needed to work for his father, but when he heard Danner's explanation, his eyes rounded with surprise. He raised his head, and looked at his older cousin as he scratched his head. "That's a scary thought," he murmured.

Danner grinned. "Not really. Think of it like this; My name is Christoff Prouter, and saving the family business is what I do."

Christoff laughed. "Remind me of that when I get there," he said when he finally got over his amusement.

Danner slapped his cousin lightly on the back as he nodded. He then went to his room.

He took off his boots, socks, and pants, then laid back on the on the pillows with a sigh. It had been a long Halloween day, and he was glad it was over. With some reluctance, he set up and grabbed the knit blanket at foot of the bed. He then laid back down and spread it on top of him.

"Goodnight Dad. Goodnight Mom," he said as he closed his eyes.

The End

Magical Retribution

In Another Time And Another Land

Part 1

Magic is Born

They were born on All Hallow's Eve and minutes apart, and though twins, they were not alike. One baby girl's hair was blond and curly, and her eyes were sky blue. The other baby's hair was black with no curl, and her eyes were pale gray. The midwife gasped when she saw the mage marks tattooed on their shoulders.

"Leave us!" Lady Mintera commanded.

Once the woman was gone, Mintera bent over the girls and examined their bodies. "They are marked on their shoulders with a crescent moon. Both will be mages. The fair one's mark is silver. The dark-haired one has a blue moon," she told her daughter. "I will notify Damus his children are born."

"No!" Syanne declared emotionally.

"They were never yours, Sy. You knew that the day your father took the marriage price in gold. Lord Damus paid for a child. Now, he will get two."

"Sy looked over at her children, her heart heavy with grief. "He paid for a child, and that is all he gets. I am taking one with me."

"You have no place to live but here," Mintera protested.

"There is another who cares for me more than you and Father do."

"You will bring disaster down on all our heads with your stubbornness, Sy," Mintera complained, knowing the girl was going to her grandfather's home in the mountains, two days ride from Allistar.

"He gets his child. The deal between him and Father is completed. Pick one and begone! Or I will take them both with me," Syanne snapped.

Mintera looked at her daughter's tear-streaked face, then at the two sleeping children. "I told your father not to sell you to the mage, but he did," she said, fighting back the urge to weep as she stared down at the babies. Remember Sy. This is not my fault, but at the same time, I do not want to die for it either. I choose the one with black hair and gray eyes. There will be no doubt about who the child belongs to as she has the same hair and eye color as Lord Damus. We will not name her. Her father can do that."

"My daughter's name is Lana Mintera," Syanne murmured, rising from the bed and gathering the baby with hair the same color of hair and eyes that she had.

Mintera's face showed her surprise. "Thank you," she whispered emotionally.

"Mother, I may be angry with you at the moment, but I know you share no blame in the deal Father struck with Cedric."

Mintera put a hand over her eyes to cover her tears, then scolded herself. There was no time to grieve. Syanne needed to leave. Hartle had sent notice to Lord Damus that the birthing had begun.

"Get dressed and pack what you can for you and the babe. Also, take two of your heaviest cloaks with you. The trip will be cold. You can use one cloak to cover the baby and Hestra."

"Hestra?" Syanne questioned as she laid the baby in the cradle and picked up her other daughter. "I love you," she whispered fiercely, then laid her back down, swallowing the urge to pick her back up and run.

"Yes, you are going to need help. You can take the old mare and the goat cart. You are in no condition to walk right now. You will make yourself sick. Hestra is a good girl and not shy when it comes to chores."

Syanne looked at her mother. "Why don't you come with me? Grandfather has room for us both."

"My place is here, Sy," Mintera knew that if she left, Hartle would hunt them down. "Now, I had better find Hestra and tell her to pack her things. Then I need to go wake Thom and have him ready the cart for you. Your father can send someone to bring the mare and cart back if he wants it back."

* * *

When Hestra volunteered to drive the cart, Syanne handed her a cloak to wear. It was still several hours before dawn, and the air was damp and cold. She climbed up on the bench and took the basket with the baby from Thom. "Take us out here very slow, Hestra. We do not want Father to hear us leaving," she said as she used a cord to secure a basket handle to a small iron ring hanging off one of the bench's back slats.

"No lights came on as they moved past the house and onto the road. "Take the north fork when you come to it," Syanne told the girl, leaning back against the wooden slats.

She closed her eyes once they were on the road and drifted toward sleep but was flung sideways when the cart hit a deep rut.

Hestra stopped the cart when she saw her mistress struggling to sit upright. "Sorry, Mistress. I cannot see the rain gullies in the dark."

"It is not your fault, Hestra. I would not have seen it either. In the meantime, we both had better fasten ourselves to one of the slats." Syanne said, standing up and grabbing two leather belts hanging off a hook attached to the top slat and handing the girl one of them. "The sun will be rising in a couple of hours. The ride will get easier, then. There is a small stream about three or four hours up the road. When you see it, pull off and move us behind the trees. We will take a break and have a bite to eat."

"Yes, Mistress," Hestra said as she pulled a rope through a slat and tied it around her waist.

As the cart began moving, Syanne reached over and touched her daughter. Her warm little body told her all was well. She leaned back against the slats and closed her eyes but did not try to sleep as the cart pitched one way then the other every time it hit a gully wash in the road. Once the sun was up, the ride was smoother, and she fell asleep. She woke when she heard Lana fussing.

"She seems to know that it is time to eat, Mistress," Hestra said as she pulled the reins to turn the cart and followed the well-worn path that led to the trees.

Part 2

Blood Fever

Syanne felt tears in her eyes when she saw smoke drifting from the chimney of her Grandfather's home. She knew she was near collapse. She also felt feverish. She pulled up in front of the door. "Stay on the bench, Hestra! Grandfather has dogs that bite," she told the girl.

"Grandfather!" She called out.

Hestra was surprised by the size of the two-story stone house. It was as large as most palaces in Allistar, but there were no walls around it. She saw a tall man with silver hair step out the door and whistle. She gasped and pulled her feet beneath her skirt when she saw a black bear come running around the side of the house.

"Jak, the one with yellow hair, is my granddaughter. The other one is a friend. They mean us no harm." Gilandar told the bear.

"What happened to the dogs?" Syanne asked as she struggled to untie the basket.

"Lost them to wolves three winters ago. Found Jak while hunting for them. Hunters had killed his mother. They were going to kill him too, but I persuaded them to give him to me."

Syanne nodded. Her grandfather was a mage. It would not have taken much persuasion to convince them to give him the bear.

"Of course, Jak is not an average bear. He has magic and can make himself invisible. That said, what are you doing here? Wait! Don't tell me. Let me find out for myself."

Syanne sat still while her grandfather probed her mind.

Gilander spat out a curse when he found what had been done to her. "Your Father always did value gold more than life. That is why I live here, and he lives in Allistar. "Hand me the basket with the babe in it. I need to tell Jak how important she is."

Syanne handed the basket to her grandfather and climbed down off the cart. She felt her knees give way and would have fallen if Hestra had not come to her aid and propped her up with her own body.

Gilander, seeing his granddaughter was not well, set the basket on the ground. Take the child into the house, Jak, while I tend to Syanne.

Hestra's eyes grew wide as she watched the bear stand on his hind legs, take the basket into a paw, and start for the house. *He truly is a magical bear*, she thought.

Syanne gave her grandfather a tearful smile. "Sorry, I am not feeling well," she apologized.

"*Kernal!*" Gilandar called out with his mind for the young man living in the barn. "*I need your help. I am in the front yard.*"

"This is my granddaughter, Syanne," Gilandar told Kernal as the young man walked up. "Help me get her inside. She is sick."

Kernal motioned for Gilandar to move aside. He then smiled at Hestra. "You can let go of her now. I have a hold of her."

With the ease of a mountain youth, Kernal picked Syanne up and carried her into the house."

"Put her in the guest room by the kitchen!" Gilander called out. "What's your name?" He asked the young girl who had come with Syanne.

"Hestra Picket, my lord. Recently kitchen girl, and now maid and nanny for Lady Syanne," she proudly announced.

"Well then, Hestra, follow me. You can take care of the child while I take care of Syanne. You do know how to care for a baby, don't you?"

"I do, sire. But I have no way to feed her."

"I have small milk pouches. I use them to feed my animals when needed. We also have fresh goat milk in the pantry. That should take care of feeding the baby. Fruity is my cook. She will get what you need."

Hestra entered the house and looked around for the basket with the baby. She saw the bear sitting beside it, looking at the child. She swallowed nervously. "Could you get her for me, sire?"

As Gilandar reached for the baby, the bear growled.

"Now, Jak. The baby's wetcloth needs changing, and she needs to be fed. You cannot do that, and neither can I, but Hestra can. You can guard her while she sleeps or talk to her when she is awake. She might not understand you because she is young and doesn't know words yet, but she will listen to you. Also, if I am not mistaken, she has magic but is too young to understand that."

Jak knew the girl had magic and could speak, but at her request, he kept that to himself. He got to his feet and went to look at Hestra. *"Take good care of her,"* he said, speaking to the girl's mind.

"I will, Lord Jak," Hestra said, bowing before the bear.

Jak nodded. He then turned and went outside. He was hungry too, and there were fish in the nearby stream.

* * *

Gillander did what he could for Syanne but knew it was not enough. She was dying, and there was only one mage who might be able to save her. He got up and went outside and called for Jak. He would need the bear's magic to take him to Allistar. The question of who got the baby he would deal with later.

* * *

Cedric Dumas reached for his wand when he saw the bear and man appear in his bedchamber. When he saw it was Lord Gilandar Bannerstone, he lowered his wand but did not put it away.

"I come in peace, Cedric. I need your help. Syanne is dying, and you are the only one I know who can stave off death."

Cedric put his wand down and rose from his chair. "Where is she?" He asked.

"My house. If you will come and grab hold of one of those chain loops on Jak's collar, we can be there within a few seconds."

"Seconds," Cedric questioned skeptically.

"Yes, my bear, Jak, has magic. Between the two of us, we came up with a travel spell. You will be safe enough if that is what's worrying you."

Cedric shook his head. "I am not worried. I was surprised by your claim. Give me a few minutes to get my boots on, tell my housekeeper I am leaving, and grab my potion bag. Also, I need to check on my daughter and let her nursemaid know I will be gone for a few days."

"I guess this is as good a time as any to ask if you are aware you have another daughter. Two girls were born, not one."

"Yes. I know. The midwife came and told me. I was relieved to know that Syanne would not be left childless or feel forced to come and live with me to be with her children."

"Then you do care for her.?"

"Yes, I do. However, when Sy found out her father charged me a wedding price, she packed her clothes and went back home."

"Who told her about the wedding price?"

"Her father. When he found out she was with child, he told her about the marriage price I paid for her, which was his doing, not mine."

Gilandar shook his head in disgust. His son never would learn to keep his mouth shut.

"I will be right back," Cedric said as he finished pulling his boots on and stood.

* * *

Cedric put a hand on Syanne's forehead and closed his eyes. He found what he feared most. The fever had poisoned her blood, and her lungs rattled with fluid. He removed his hand from her forehead and looked at Gilandar. "I will do what I can, but she has blood fever.

"What is blood fever?" Jak asked when he saw Gilandar's face lose color.

Cedric's mouth dropped open. "Did that bear speak to me? He asked.

Gilandar nodded. "He probably speaks better than most do. He reads too."

"Blood fever is when an infection enters the blood and poisons it. The kidneys shut down, and the lungs fill up." Cedric answered.

"How do you fix it?" the bear asked.

"There is only one thing I know that will cure blood fever—*Zibatti* pollen. I have a bit with me, but only two or three doses, which will not be enough to cure her."

Jak watched Lord Dumas take a bottle out of his bag and a tiny spoon. He then poured some yellow powder into the spoon and fed it to the young woman. "

"I will give her another spoonful every two hours until I run out," Cedric told Gilandar.

"Where can you get more?" Jak asked.

"It grows in Elf country. The only other in this land that might have some is Mother Candle. She is an ancient healer that lives in a cave on Burnt Mountain. Ten days ride from here."

"It's only a few seconds away with Jak," Gilandar stated.

"I did not bring any gold with me," Cedric said.

Gilandar reached into his tunic pocket and took out a bag of coins. "Take these with you. Syanne is worth more to me than gold."

"I will use what I need but will repay you. She is my wife, and it is my responsibility to see to her care," Cedric declared.

"Do as you will and can. But you will find those are not your average coins. Those are Dragon Crowns from the land of Angland. Each with a value of ten crowns in this land."

Cedric opened the pouch and took out a coin. It was larger and thicker than any gold piece he had ever seen. "When I get back, and Syanne is on her way to recovery, I would like to hear how you came by these coins."

Gilandar chuckled. "Now that is a story to be remembered. Jak will enjoy it too."

Jak sat down and looked at his friend.

"Not now, Jak. You need to take Cedric to see Mother Candle. When you return, I will tell you and Cedric the story."

Jak got to his feet and looked at Cedric.

"Do you know the way to Burnt Mountain?" The mage asked.

"I have never been there, but I have studied all of Gilandar's maps. I only need to wish myself there, and there is where we will go," Jak replied.

Cedric nodded and walked over and grabbed hold of one of the loops on Jak's collar.

Part 3

Mother Candle

Cedric found himself and the bear standing on a ledge of an old dormant volcano. The ground was several hundred feet below them. He stood ready to chant a floating spell should they lose their balance.

"We are looking for Mother Candle. We need help," Jak broadcasted with his mind.

A rock in front of them slid open, revealing a cave.

As Jak entered and started down the tunnel, Cedric followed him, grateful for the candles that lit the way. The floor was smooth but not always level.

Jak stopped to look around as he came to a large room. He saw a woman with long silver braids sitting on a stone chair, watching him with eyes the color of the clouds in the sky. He moved toward her and sat down in front of her.

"We mean you no harm," Cedric said as he stood before the ancient one with eyes the color of snow and matted gray hair. He then introduced himself and the bear.

"What brings you here, mage?" Candle asked.

"My wife is dying of blood fever. I am hoping you have *Zibatti* pollen to sell."

Mother Candle's eyes went back to the bear. "You are not a simple-minded animal, are you?"

"No. I am a ghost bear, and I have magic.'

"But you are not a ghost?"

"I am called a ghost bear because I can make myself invisible."

"Interesting. I have never heard of your kind."

"Most have not, but my companion knew what I was the minute he laid eyes on me. He saved me from those who killed my mother."

Candle's eyes moved to the mage. "I do have *Zibatti* pollen, but it is expensive. It has taken me three years to fill one bottle."

"I have gold with me," Cedric declared. "Name your price."

"A hundred crowns," Candle said. She watched as the mage brought out a coin purse. *Humph*! she thought. *He does not argue the price.*

"Does that make a difference?" Jak asked. *"If it does, I can argue for him as it is my friend's gold. Though, to be fair, Cedric has offered to pay it back."*

Candle looked at the bear. *"And a good friend you are. The gold means nothing to me. But it is the only thing traders will take. One has to eat, you know?"*

Jak nodded. He understood. Gilandar complained loudly and often when he dealt with traders.

Cedric counted out ten coins and handed them to the woman. He then waited to explain their value.

Candle took the coins and was surprised by their weight. When she saw the front of one, her brow went up. "Where did you get this dragon gold?" she asked.

"From my wife's grandfather, Lord Gilandar Bannerstone," Cedric answered, surprised that she recognized the origin of the coins.

Candle clamped her jaw shut to keep it from falling open. Long had she sought news of her beloved Gilandar. She rose from her chair and went over to a stack of shelves with front guards that kept the bottles from falling off the shelves when the ground rumbled, shaking the ground beneath the cave, which was happening more often these past few months.

She pulled a leather bag with handles from one shelf and began to pack it with bottles. When it was full, she motioned for the mage to come and take it.

Cedric took the bag from her, then watched her empty the shelves as she filled two more bags and another with dried herbs.

Candle then went to a cupboard and packed a bag of clothing, shoes, and other things. When finished, she retrieved a short leather rope from a niche in the stone wall.

"I am going back with you, Jak. I assume you can carry me and my things as well."

In answer, a saddle box appeared on Jak's back.

Candle packed her belongings. As she straightened up, the dragon coins in her pocket clinked as they rolled back the other way. She pulled them out of her pocket, stuck one back in, and handed the others to Cedric. "I will keep one. Not as payment, but as a souvenir of the time Gilandar and I spent in Angland."

Cedric's brow went up before he thanked her.

"Can we go from here, Mother Candle, or do we need to move outside?" Jak asked.

"Outside.," Candle answered. I have wards on this cave that might interfere with your magic."

Jak turned around and started for the cave's entrance.

Part 4

Magical Retribution

When they materialized in Gilandar's front yard, Cedric turned to look at Mother Candle, and his mouth dropped open with surprise. The woman was not young, but she was now not ancient either and her eyes were now blue, not white.

"My name is Candle Wickenberg." When Cedric smiled, she nodded. "My father had a sense of humor. My brother was born in a barn, and he named him Rafter. As for me, Mother Candle is an illusion I use to protect myself from the bandits and other low life that would take advantage of a woman living alone. Not that I was ever in danger from them, but I dislike killing others, even if they are scoundrels. It also keeps people from lining up at my door, wanting one thing or another. I allowed you access because I sensed the magic in both of you, and that intrigued me. Mages rarely come to visit me."

Cedric made no reply but could not help but think about the cave's door. Both he and Candle had to hold onto Jak's collar rings to keep from falling off the ledge.

Jak listened to Candle. Like her, he did not like bandits.

"Candle! Is that you?" Gilandar asked as he came out the door and saw the woman standing with Jak and Cedric.

"Yes, Gil, it is me," Candle replied as she used a spell to keep herself from bawling like a babe upon seeing the only man she had ever loved.

Gilandar hurried over and hugged her. "I thought you were dead," he said, tears in his eyes.

"And I thought you dead too, but I kept hope in my heart," Candle said, her eyes tearing up despite the emotional spell she had cast.

"That is probably what saved me," Gilandar said as he stepped away.

"Candle and I were to be married when we were young, but fate sent us separate ways," he explained to Cedric when he saw the mage staring at them.

"But enough of us, We can catch up later. Syanne is burning up with a fever, and her breathing is ragged. Did you bring the *Zibatti* pollen?"

"Yes," said Candle as she undid the latch on Jak's saddle bag and pulled one of the bags out. "If you could bring in the other two medicine bags, Cedric. I would appreciate it."

Gilandar saw Kernal in the barn doorway, watching them. "Come help bring in Candle's bags. You can put them upstairs in the bedchamber across from mine."

Before Candle examined the young woman, she took a small pottery bowl and a bottle of rye spirits from her bag. She uncorked the whiskey and set it down on the table but kept the bowl in her hand. She walked over to the bed, leaned over, and put her hand on the young woman's forehead. She found the poison that was turning the girl's blood black. She closed her eyes and chanted a spell that would let her extract the worst of it. A few seconds later, she spat a blob of black tar into the bowl. She then reached for the bottle of rye spirits, took a swig, and rinsed her mouth with it.

"Hopefully, that will give the *Zibatti* time to start the healing process," she told Gilandar and Cedric, who were staring at her with slack mouths. Neither one had ever seen anyone do what she just did.

"I hope we paid you enough to do that. It won't poison you, will it?" Gilandar questioned.

"No. I did not swallow any of it. That is why I held the bowl. The Rye kills the poison and cleanses my mouth. Now I need to give her a double dose of the pollen."

When finished, Candle looked around the room. "I need a sitting chair brought in as I intend to spend the night with her. If she makes it through this night, we can hope the worst is over. I will do my best to save her, Gilandar. I know how much she means to you and the mage."

As Candle saw the mage hand Gilandar a bag of coins, she added, "I took one of your dragon coins as a souvenir of our time spent in Angland, Gil. I want no payment for saving your granddaughter, other than the room upstairs. Burnt Mountain is about ready to erupt again. I will not be going back there."

"Consider it a deal, Candle. Long have I looked for you," Gilandar said before turning to look at Kernal. "Could you bring the green sitting chair and footstool in from the day room? It is the most comfortable one for sitting. Also, tell Fruity there will be one more person living here, and Mage Cedric will be here for a while too."

When he saw Candle and Cedric looking at him, he explained, "Fruity is my cook. Her daughter Kayna keeps the house clean and does the laundry. Kernal and Kayna are married and live in the barn house. He tends to the goats, gathers firewood, and does whatever else needs to be done. Jak does most of the sweeping and dusting, using bear magic. I try to keep out of their way."

* * *

Syanne opened her eyes and saw a woman standing over her. "Where am I?" She asked as she swallowed to ease her dry throat.

"You are in your Grandfather's house," Candle replied. "I will go tell him you are awake. He has been worried about you."

As Candle went out the door to find Gilandar, Syanne tried to sit up but found herself so weak she could not rise, "How long have I been here?" she wondered.

"Six days," a man's voice said.

Syanne turned her head. When she saw Cedric, she gasped and started wheezing.

Cedric moved to lift her up and pat her on the back. "Do not be afraid of me, Sy. I am not here to take your child. I am here to help you live."

"Promise me," Syanne whispered. She began to cry, which made the wheezing worse.

"I would never willingly harm you, Sy. Though it breaks my heart to say this, you can have Izana back if that is what your heart desires."

"She's yours. You paid for her."

"I never paid for a child, Syanne. When I went to ask Hartle if I could court you, he insisted on a bride price right then and there, telling me Lord Benton had already made an offer to marry you. He then told me he would make the wedding arrangements. When I questioned him whether that would suit you, he said you had already agreed to marry me. When you ran away, I should have gone after you, but I felt wronged by both you and your father. I love you, Syanne. I know. I never told you that. I worried it would make me look weak. But I realized how foolish I had been when I came here and found you dying."

Syanne buried her head against his chest. "When Father told me I was to marry you, I was happy as I liked you, and eventually, I began to love you. When he found out I was with child, he came by the house and told me his part of the bargain was completed. I asked him what he meant by that, and he said you would get the child you paid for." He then laughed before asking, 'Did you think it was your worthless hide he wanted?' That is why I ran back home," Syanne said, tears running down her cheeks.

Gilandar had stopped at the door to give his granddaughter time to make peace with her husband. When he heard what Hartle had done, he spat out a curse.

Candle patted him on the shoulder. "Anger is bad for your health," she murmured.

Cedric felt Syanne's body go limp. He looked over at Gilandar and Candle.

"I think she fainted," he told them as he laid her back down.

Candle went and put a hand to her forehead. "Yes. It seems she has. But the fever is gone. I will stay here with her. You two need to go make that disgusting man dribble in his pants."

Cedric's brow went up as he stared at the healer.

"I would, but Hartle is my son," Candle."

"Ah. That does make it difficult," Candle said, nodding.

"Grandfather," Syanne whispered.

Gilandar walked over and took his granddaughter's hand into his. He noticed the cracks in the skin on her hands. He could not see her arms, legs, or her feet as they beneath blanket, but he knew they were probably cracked as well. Blood fever was a wicked illness. He would ask Candle later what they could do to make sure the cracking did not leave scars.

"Don't hurt Father. I could not bear the guilt of knowing I was to blame for that."

"I am not going to hurt him, Sy. I think he has done a good job of that himself. But I am going to ask your mother to come and live here with me. I don't want Hartle taking his anger out on her."

Gilandar saw her try to nod, but her eyes closed. He laid her hand at her side. "Better we go talk elsewhere. She needs to rest."

"I will stay and keep watch," Cedric said. I can read my book at the same time. You don't need me to talk to Mintera."

"No, but your presence might keep Hartle silent," Gilandar said, not looking forward to giving his son the tongue lashing he deserved.

"Take Mother Candle with you. Once he sees her and Jak, he won't be arguing with you."

Gilandar nodded, then grinned when he saw Candle turn into an old crone with white eyes.

* * *

Mintera gasped when Gilandar, an old woman, and a bear appeared in her sitting room.

"Do not be afraid, Mintera," Gilandar told her, frowning when he saw her eye was swollen and blackened. "We come in peace, or at least we are in peace with you. Hartle, not so much. I see he has been beating on you."

Mintera got to her feet. "Is Sy and the baby okay?" She asked.

"The baby is fine. Syanne would have died of blood fever had Candle not come and healed her. It will take weeks or months before she completely recovers," Gilandar replied.

"I should not have let go," Mintera said, tears running down her face.

Gilandar shook his head. "It is not your fault she left. Hartle is the one to blame. I would like you to come live with us, Mintera. It is no longer safe here for you, and Syanne needs you."

"Candle will help you pack while I go tell Hartle what I think of him. I doubt it will change anything, but it needs to be said."

"He might hit you," Mintera warned.

"Well, he can try, but then Jak will have to sit on him."

Jak looked at Mintera, nodded, then growled, bared his teeth, and sat down with a *whump*.

Mintera chuckled. "Thank you, Jak. I think you and I are going to be good friends."

Jak got to his feet and bowed.

* * *

Gilandar told Hartle how disappointed he was in him, and that his lies and greed had almost cost Syanne her life.

Hartle stood there glaring at him. "I am not a bit sorry for anything I did. A person has to be strong in today's world," he declared

"Maybe with outsiders, but not with your own family. Mintera has a blackened eye. What is your excuse for that?'

"A man's got a right to teach his woman manners, Hartle responded churlishly. "If she doesn't like it, then she can get out!"

"Well, that is just what she is going to do. I am taking her to my home. It is obvious that she is not safe for her in this house anymore." As Hartle opened his mouth to protest, Gilandar added. "Let me tell you something, boy. This estate belongs to me, and so does the title of Lord Bannerstone. That I chose to lend it to you does not mean I cannot take it away. If I catch you harming one more person that does not deserve it, you will be publicly disinherited, and out on the street. Understand?"

Hartle's face lost color as he realized his father was not making an idle threat. He cast him a blistering look but nevertheless nodded.

Gilandar's eyes caught movement coming through the door and turned to look. His brow went up when he saw a crystal pitcher of water come flying into the room, heading straight for Hartle. Before he could react, the pitcher dumped the water on his son's head, then fell onto the carpet, but did not break.

"There was no need to do that," Hartle sputtered, wiping water from his eyes.

"I didn't do it, but I would not mind shaking the hand of the one that did."

"*Candle must have done that?*" he told Jak.

"*Nope. It was Lana. When I told her what Candle said, she asked me what dribble meant. I told her wet pants.*"

"She spoke to you?" Gilandar questioned, so surprised by Jak's words that he spoke aloud.

"*Yes. She speaks perfect Bearish,*" Jak answered.

"Who spoke to me?" Hartle asked, looking around the room nervously.

"No one spoke to you, Hartle. All I can say is you had better change your ways. You have two granddaughters that will make your life miserable if you don't."

* * *

Hestra was folding wetcloths when she heard what sounded like laughter coming from the baby's basket. She hurried over to make sure the child was not choking. She gasped when she saw the baby looking at her with glowing eyes and a smile on her face.

The End

Get your copy today of **Dragon Child of Angland**; the story of what happens after Pumpkin becomes a prince and has more enemies than he can handle.
Now available on Amazon.

www.ingramcontent.com/pod-product-compliance
Lightning Source LLC
Chambersburg PA
CBHW070503130626
46555CB00003B/1134